Kite Strings

By

Monica C. Petter

First published by Monica C. Petter

ISBN: 978-0-578-07129-9

Printed by Instantpublisher.com

Cover Art © Monica C. Petter

Dedication

"I can still remember the piercing, unblinking blue eyes of a teacher who could look right through me, and see every vacuum of knowledge I so desperately tried to cover up in class." ~Unknown

Mentors inspire, guide, and challenge life's shades of gray.

For

NJB

Special thanks to all my readers...
And those shadows in my life that floated in for a
 reason, a season and a lifetime....

All my love to David and Blondie...
For letting me pour time into these pages...

Madison Peacock

Empty Houses
April 2008

The trees have grown so much in the past ten years. I remember when Rhett and I moved into the house, they were young and fragile, blown about easily by storms. Now, when the winds come, the trunks hold firm and steadfast. The arms sway rather romantically, seasoned and deeply rooted into place. They are beginning to open fresh, lime green leaves that are almost transparent. All the other colorful perennials we planted years ago are out in full color. There was a shower this morning that left everything sweet and earthy like fresh garden dirt. I notice the daffodils have already bloomed. They always begin emerging in March. I dug up some of our daffodils and planted them on Rhett's burial plot. They were our favorite flower. I've now left our mark for a thousand springs. Our life together not forgotten. But, that was another life. I am now another man's wife. I don't plan to visit his grave anymore.

The rhythmic thumps of raindrops bounce off the empty house and echo like a pinball. The hollow tone reminds me of that deep baritone sound when something is missing. My footsteps and the rain complement each other as I walk into the living room. The wooden floors we refinished are so beautiful. I sit on the window sill and gaze up at the vaulted ceiling as the rain cascades off the skylights. I remember dreaming here ten years ago with a man whose star burned out too quickly by his own hand. We were mapping out our life. Ten years ago, I saw forever in his smile. I knew which room would be our child's room. A child I never had. Dreams roughed out on paper, but never realized. Thrown in trashcans for good reasons, silent reasons understood only by a husband and wife. Spouses speak in code, their own language. My relationship was no different. At times, real speaking was nothing more than the quiet erasing of our plans - the slow unraveling of a life one thread at a time.

The house is empty and naked, not really a home anymore. I feel disconnected as if I don't recognize it without its substance. Without our things, it is wood and sheetrock, colors with no character. I wonder what this house will say to its new owners. I wonder if it will keep my secrets. I feel it saying goodbye to me as I walk from room to room. I left many things behind – bits of my heart in the closet corner, pieces of my pride left in the back of a bathroom drawer, crumbs of denial on the kitchen counter. My soul's story of grief can only be revealed when the rain and southern humidity fog the windows.

My old life flashes before me and disappears in a blip. My past and my future now tethered by the love of a child not my own. The fact I am wearing a new wedding ring represents one life lost so another could be found. In any end, there is always a beginning. What lies ahead can only be understood in what was left behind. I didn't want to love again. I didn't need love I couldn't control. But, life is what you learn from the pain and love isn't about trepidation or control. I run toward life less fearful of the uncertainties. Like an eager child running with scissors, I chance to fall and get hurt... but in the end, I'd still rather run.

Beginning of the End
May into June 2007

Madison had found Rhett slumped over his desk, face down in a pool of his own blood and brains. His Little Rock law office was now bright red blood spattered art complimenting the vibrant green of May. The bullet had entered his chin and exited the top right side of his head, negating all his years of law school. He was alive, but in a coma. From the bullet's trajectory, the doctors suspected suicide. Madison suspected family.

Dyer stood in the Rhett's hospital room doorway. Madison had been grief counseling Dyer Brown and his five- year-old daughter, Hannah, for the past six months. He had lost his wife suddenly and was now reliving his own tragedy.

She silently noticed how every hospital had that foul, metallic smell. It smelled of death and bed rest. As she walked out of the room into the hospital hallway that echoed with strangers' voices,

5

she was reminded of her mortality and how quickly it can be snuffed out. Madison's heels could be heard clicking on the tile as they walked down the long, cold corridor. She wiped tears and Dyer grabbed a few tissues from the nurse's station as he passed, handing them to her. She pushed past Dyer, trying to hide her tears. Dyer grabbed her shoulder.

"Don't – I need some air."

Dyer knew nothing about Madison's life, only what was missing from it. She cut her crystal eyes at him firmly. He saw dark rage cloaked and it gave him a shudder.

Spring was aging. The late May afternoon humidity rushed their faces as they stepped outside the hospital. They sat on a park bench under a huge oak tree. He waltzed into her defensive personal space, reaching for her hands and pulling her tightly laced fingers apart.
"You can lean on me, Madison."

Dyer's pity for her situation only made Madison churn with guilt.

"That's how I got here…leaning into you and Hannah…if I hadn't been with you two at the zoo..."

"You were filling a hole."

Dyer noticed her blood-stained cuticles. He held them delicately as if they were made of paper. His hands gentle for a man who slung boards and hammers for a living.

"Whose hole…Hannah's or mine?"

He just smiled at her, kissing her softly on the cheek. Madison found the lines very blurry between them.

Rhett Peacock

Rhett had been a man who dressed to the nines and whitened his teeth. His hair had always fallen almost gracefully across his face. The bullet had taken out a chunk of his skull. His perfectly combed locks of golden hair were gone, shaved for the surgery and bandages. His pallor now matched those fencerow-whitened teeth he had just had done a few months ago.

7

Madison knew Rhett had been far from suicidal. His greed had been the catalyst that created the great cavern which simply moved them to quiet resolution. The bandages hopefully signified the end of his manipulation. Tyranny had been replaced with apathy.

Rhett slept bandaged and unaware in his blue checkered hospital gown. He would have balked at the flimsy cotton fabric. Madison balked at his reversal. Her illusions of their marriage had mimicked smoke dancing rather hypnotically around her until it clouded her vision. She feared he would unroll all their years of dirt in a soul-purging tyranny. Bullets did strange things. Madison rubbed her weary temples. Secrets had painfully eroded their sleep over the past ten years. She sat now no further than a foot from her husband, noticing how the blood stains still tattooed the fine lines of his cheeks. They matched the ones on Madison's cuticles and under her fingernails she could never seem to scrub away.

Just die she whispered in Rhett's bandaged ear. She hoped those words ricocheted off the bareness of his wounded skull. Rhett's eyes fluttered, opening. He looked straight ahead, trying to focus. The clock ticked loudly on the wall beside her. Her future hung in mid-air, a coin toss spinning over and over, waiting to land. They locked eyes for a long millisecond. Rhett studied her mouth; his mannerisms similar. Something very original passed between them.

"*Die*…and miss all the fun?"

Rhett merely grimaced. He did not look at her. Madison's heart jumped out of her chest with a familiar fear she had sheltered since the beginning of this nightmare. Rhett's soul hadn't flown skyward with the bullet that exited his brain. As drool ran out and down the side of Rhett's mouth, Madison covered her own, nauseous. She had an urge to run far, far away. Evasiveness was their specialty. It was easy as wading into a cool swimming pool on a humid July day.

9

Dirty Laundry

Rhett spent his June birthday awake, but unresponsive.   The steady stream of calls ended. Rhett's family had never been bonded by their shared DNA. Madison felt more like a guard than a concerned wife. She had requested no visitors after his uncle had stopped by once or twice when she wasn't there. Madison had been in a perpetual holding pattern regarding Rhett's business affairs. She wished death upon him daily.

Madison's facial commands were mastered. A reflex so ingrained, she ordered her feelings behind a smile. Her anxious strides could be heard clicking on the shiny floor of the hospital as she made her way down a silent hallway toward Rhett's room. He had been downgraded from critical condition. His new room was a softer color, a creamy butter yellow.

Rhett looked small as he lay in the large new bed. He was more alert, yet suspiciously quiet the past week. His mood had soured the past twenty-four hours. Madison reached for his hand and she felt her face flush, their fingers a telepathic line between them. Her stomach seized.

"Why do you keep coming here?"

Rhett's eyes were closed, yet his mouth snarled arrogantly. The sky could be falling, knocking him to the gates of hell and he would flip the devil the bird.

"Open your damn eyes. I know you remember me."

"You're my wife."

"What else aren't you sharing?"

"We liked flying kites."

"*You* liked kites."

Rhett flipped, turning his back to Madison. He was no more than a petulant child patronizing her. He reached in his nightstand drawer, pulling out pictures of Madison and Dyer walking hand in hand with Hannah at the zoo, Dyer with his arm around Madison as Hannah sat on her lap. It was apparent Rhett's uncle Vincent had paid him a visit despite her best efforts to keep him away.

"Why should I tell you anything? You don't care about me anymore."

Rhett could make her feel guilty for breathing other people's air. He was a jealous man who didn't share his things, especially his wife.

Madison took the pictures from his weak hands and examined them. Rhett and Madison spoke in code with their eyes; nonverbal communication was the foundation of their marriage. They couldn't lie to each other.

"If you remember anything about our life, you wouldn't be asking me to explain these photos."

Madison felt her neck hot with anger again. Rhett studied her downturned mouth before speaking.

"You need to stay away from them…quit playing house with *this* man."

Rhett hated Lane for recommending Madison's counsel to the Browns.

"You are a real son of a bitch. I'm tired of hating you."

Madison crumpled the photos, throwing them one by one at Rhett. She had hated hanging from his hip like a handgun. He'd pull her out of his holster and shoot her into a crowd, blowing the smoke she caused, smiling his shit-eaten grin and putting her back into place. Without Rhett, Madison was more tightly collected, stacked almost perfectly like a fresh deck of cards.

Go Fly a Kite
July 2007

Rhett's condition had not changed as a few more weeks slipped by uneventfully. He slept most of the time, not talking to her. Rhett's calculated manipulation appeared in the form of childlike pouting. When he did look at Madison, his mouth turned pensive. His gaze seemed almost malicious. His uncooperative moods were selfish and spiteful.

She turned her wedding ring over and over on her finger, unscrewing her past slowly, painfully. Madison hadn't flown a

13

kite since she was a kid. Rhett had taken her to a large hay field just outside of Little Rock on a windy March day some twelve years ago to fly a kite he had constructed. He loved building kites and manipulating them from a string. Now he couldn't tie his shoe.

Her ring finger was raw. Rhett moaned inaudibly. Madison left the hospital and drove to the open field where they had flown that kite. The hay was gone and construction had begun on a subdivision of new homes on the land that adjoined the Arkansas River. The humidity stifled, making her clothes cling to her skin.

Madison drove down the newly paved road. No new houses had been built, only the road that led to the river. Potential surrounded her just as it had all those years ago with Rhett. When she got to the end of the road, she stopped her car and stepped into the warm midmorning sunlight. She didn't have a kite today, so she walked to the water's edge. *Look at it go, baby. Just like you and me.* She remembered Rhett's

14

deep, southern intonation. They had flown the kite and watched it dance on the wind before crashing into bits. She fell in love with his control and abandon in that moment. He kissed her. When she looked up into his eyes, he studied her, calculating her potential. It was the same sort of look that had lingered in Rhett's last morning kiss. His eyes were suspicious, laced with foreshadowed guilt for what he was about to do with her naivety.

Madison looked up at the blueness of the jet streams that darted and dashed. She had been betrayed by her heart. Anger brewed. Grief turned her bully. She looked at the wedding band on her finger. It was a giant diamond that stood for nothing. She worked the ring off her finger, screaming obscenities as she threw it into the river.

In Dyer Straits

Madison's whole body trembled as she drove back to her office. Rhett would have crapped in his silk underwear. She laughed sardonically through her tears. She had just thrown a two karat wedding ring into the river. At least now Rhett had a reason for all the misplaced spite in his glances and groans.

Dyer was her last appointment for the day. He walked into the office and noticed Madison's appearance. Her clothes were wrinkled. Her neck was flushed.

"Something happen?"

Madison ignored the question. She flipped open his chart and began reading. Her eyes were lost in an almost bipolar sorrow.

"Did you remove the rest of your wife's clothes as you had anticipated doing this weekend?"

"No. Madison, are you ok?"

Dyer picked at his calloused cuticles, remembering the blood on Madison's.

"I could give a shit right now whether you got rid of your dead wife's clothes. I just threw my wedding ring into the river."

Madison snapped his file shut, succumbing to the warm rush of crazed tears. She had never lost her composure in front of a client. But, Dyer wasn't just any client. She felt weak and infantile as she put her head down to cry. Her face was in her hands as she sobbed.

"I haven't cried in years."

"Maybe that is your problem, counselor."

Dyer found her vulnerability intriguing as a coiled snake. He motioned, embracing her. She hugged Dyer and the comfort of *this* man's arms felt different. He was the one friend Madison had.

Dyer Brown

Good Grief
July 2007

I am a builder. I start with a solid foundation. Some builders are cheap and lazy and do what is easiest and fastest. They think they can get more out of the build with less effort. A house is always tested, and shortcuts end up costing more or ruining a reputation. Then, there are those who do everything right with money no object. They build the house with steel and brick to guarantee its strength. I fall somewhere in the middle. I try to invest in the right places. The only guarantee is what I control. The weather doesn't give a damn. It can bend the strongest steel.

Grief changes a person. After finding my wife dead on the bathroom floor, it only took the blink of an eye to watch my house crumble. The only reason I survived my wife's death was because of my daughter. My wife and I fought a lot about

19

children. Actually we just fought - period. I hadn't invested as much in my marriage as I had my houses. But when we decided to adopt Hannah Beth, we called a truce. Everything was working. Then my wife died. I hated her for dying and leaving me to raise our little girl alone.

In walks Madison Peacock. I am sure on our first session I was just another asshole with bad breath. She silently watched me wallow in self-pity. With my temper, Madison has learned what to say and what to know. It is the way she handles Hannah that pulled me out of the deep end. Madison has shown me how to love my daughter. She gives Hannah a woman's love I envy and miss.

I pull into her cracked drive. They planted the trees too close. Roots are now breaking the concrete. Roots do that, take over and crack the foundation. I put her foreign car in park and she touches my hand, weaving her fingers into mine. I can tell she doesn't want to be alone tonight. I don't want to leave her. I get Madison's life even

though it is so very different from mine.
She's complicated. She keeps her sexy
mouth shut. I know she could cut my throat
with her words. She turns off the car, taking
the keys. Low rumbles grow in the distance.
The winds pick up an empty soda can and
spin it across the yard. All good builders
will tell you the sounds of wind and thunder
cause anxiety.

You Can Run

The late day sun was in Dyer's eyes as he drove Madison home from her office. It blindsided him just as Madison had that afternoon. Dyer didn't know all the gadgets on her Mercedes, wasn't paying attention to Madison as she sat silently, staring out the window. The satin trim of her bra peeped through two gaping buttons of her blouse. She was a woman who paid attention to every detail. He wondered what she had seen in a simple man like him. They were from such different worlds.

Dyer pulled into Madison's drive. Her home was large, but not overly so. Rhett had put the money into the details as Dyer would find. There was unfamiliarity in this setting for the both of them. Meetings had been formal and in an office or with Hannah in tote, a safe sanctuary with rules. Once Dyer got through the door, he kept his hands in his pockets.

The hardwood floors and marble countertops were top dollar. He understood the kind of detail that went into this home. It was an occupational hazard. As a building contractor, he had built at least two dozen in his career.

The only audible sound was the ice hitting the glass and the train's whistle blowing in on a northern breeze. Madison handed the intricately-cut crystal glass of tequila to Dyer. They didn't speak, letting the booze cut the tension. The train whistled again, nearer this time. Thunder rumbled in the distance.

Madison sat on the hearth, sipping her tequila methodically, begging it to numb her. She stared at a pile of unopened mail on the coffee table beside Rhett's reading glasses that had a film of dust covering the lenses. Madison's mascara zigzagged down her cheeks. She looked like a painted clown.

"Your face…"

There was a synchronicity, a palpable intimate sorrow they now both tasted. Dyer moved beside her on the hearth. He wiped the mascara from her cheeks with his fat thumbs. He could smell her skin and hair.

"Can I run you a bath?"

Dyer stood, offering his sweaty palm. He led her into the bedroom where Madison balled up like a child on her unmade bed. She heard the familiar, metrical sounds of the water hitting the porcelain as Dyer blindly dumped in some of her bath oils. The scent of peppermint and lavender found her nose, soothing her like a mother's lullaby. The water shut off. Madison sat up abruptly on the bed.

Dyer wiped his hands on a towel as he removed his boots. He placed them in the same spot Rhett would leave his expensive loafers each night. Construction boots walked the floors of Rhett's home with his wife. He kneeled at her level and wiped her tears with Rhett's monogrammed towel. They let their tacit chemistry speak. Madison admired his chocolate eyes as he wiped off her clownish makeup.

The train's powerful engine could be heard pulling hard up the hill. Madison was close enough that he could feel her breath on his face. Men and women define foreplay in many ways. Dyer and Madison had always verbally sparred at times. No words defined a different kind of intimacy.

Madison looked down at her buttons and then to Dyer. Her silence pleaded with him to touch her. Intimacy has no sound or design. His fingers were nimble as he unfastened each button with care. Dyer pulled her blouse off her shoulders, kissing her collarbone. Nakedness signals ultimate trust. No props or masks, just lovely skin. Her bra was satin, accentuating her full breasts. Madison sighed as Dyer kissed the top of her breast. Nakedness between lovers is frightening and erotic. She was visibly holding her breath, clenching her teeth.

"I don't know how to do *this*..."

Madison felt the train vibrating on the tracks, full steam ahead. Dyer kissed her, working his mouth wider.

"*This* is simple math, Madison."

Madison had her forearm between them. Dyer unhooked her bra, lifting

Madison and carrying her to the bath. Nakedness between friends carries volatile and strong emotions. They closed their eyes, seeing the lovers who shrouded them in guilt. Wet clothes weighted them with water and sorrow as they searched for skin, fighting against the water as they made love. Their fears masked by hints of clean lavender.

The northern breeze the night before had ushered a distant train's whistle so close that they could feel its power brush by Madison's home. The winds had accelerated, vibrating the windowpanes, waking Madison. She was lying on her side, watching the limbs on her oak tree sway like arms, the leaves' fingertips pointing at her.

Dyer lay close to her, their arms touching. The covers draped him just below his waist, revealing the sexy cut of his stomach. She watched his chest rise and fall. Raindrops began hitting the window with the force of small pebbles, intermittently washing the outside world to a blur.

Lightning highlighted Dyer's strong arms. Madison caressed them. They had held her body above him in the bath just hours earlier. Madison ran her fingertips through his thick, course hair. Guilt is not built into need's design. The hungry just can't foresee admiration becoming passionate, friends becoming lovers.

Madison's polished hardwood floor identified each step she took. She started a pot of coffee and sat in the kitchen window seat just as she had every morning. She searched her conscience for guilt, but there was none. Need is avaricious and has no conscience. She rubbed her forearms, noticing her hands. They had roamed Dyer's body like a cellist, moving her bow back and forth in crazed expression, feeling each note. Dyer was pure, cleansing the dirt and blood from her soiled existence. Had she dirtied him?

She heard his footsteps approaching. Eyes found each other and probed for walls or reasons. Dyer watched her mouth for that nervous nibble, but her lips weren't pursed or tight; they were soft, pliable, covered in his DNA. Madison saw no remorse on his face. He ran his hand through his hair, rubbing the back of his neck. That strong neck she had held onto tightly, pulling feverishly into him, his breath heavy and warm on her chest. Madison smiled, offering Dyer coffee. Her eyes offered much more. Raindrops danced down the windowpane behind her.

"Looks like rain."

Madison's eyes resembled a muddy lake on a crystal blue fall day – they reflected perfect blueness despite being soiled. Dyer poured his coffee, sharing the window seat with her. He rubbed the small of her back.

"When is our next session?"

"I don't know."

Dyer leaned into Madison, putting his lips on hers. She closed her eyes. Dyer felt a warm tear intersect their kiss.

Madison's cell phone rang from her robe pocket. The cab driver honked his horn from her driveway for Dyer. He noted her

anxiety, the haste in their goodbye.
Madison checked her voicemail. This was
the call she dreaded; the reason her guts
were knotted into orange-sized balls. It was
Rhett's uncle Vincent.

"Hello, Madison. How's my boy?
Remember, I want what is mine. You'd best
not screw me. You just can't trust anyone
these days. Betrayin' hurts....speakin'
of...I'm sendin' you some very interestin'
info. I know you feel a-l-l-l-l alone. Glad to
see you did have a friend to comfort you last
night. "

Madison threw up in her mouth a bit.
Rhett always said that snakes come to the
surface when it gets hot.

Later that morning, Madison wheeled
her car up on the curb a she pulled into her
office. Dyer observed her erratic driving,
sitting in his truck waiting for her. As if her
body knew she was safely in her office,
Madison threw up, retching loudly at the
pain, her ulcers inflamed, rejecting the
negativity. Dyer had slipped in behind her.

30

He saw her pale face and his brow furled in concern.

"It's just my ulcers."

Madison staggered to her desk, opening a prescription bottle of medication. Her eyes watered from the pain. Throwing her head back, she swallowed the pills. She picked up a chart, reviewing the next patient.

"I can't see you today."

"That phone call…I just wanted to see you."

"Here I am."

She shot a cross glare in his direction. Dyer banged his hand on her file, slamming it shut. His eyes bled confusion and anger.

"Just because you got into my pants doesn't mean you can get into my life."

He removed his fist from the file, caressing her hand, analyzing her deceptiveness. He wondered what her secrets were. She was beautifully falling apart at the seams.

Dyer closed the door to leave. With dread, Madison tore open the envelope of data Rhett's uncle Vincent had promised just an hour earlier.

Starry Blue Eyes

Madison turned the doorknob to her home, cautiously peeking around the door. She did a bug sweep and found one in her bedroom. She flushed it down the toilet. Most people wouldn't think to sweep their home for electronic bugs. Most people weren't related to Rhett's uncle.

Madison staggered to the couch, falling into it like the great abyss of her anxiety. Her chest ached hollowness. The noises of her home were heightened and rhythmic, matched only by the sound of her own breathing. A thousand voices collided thunderously at a feverish pace. The silence buzzed into nothingness. A dream sequence of her circumstances raced before her in the peaceful darkness... Rhett snarled his upper lip with ill-tempered

32

conceit…Vincent slurred his bad English over a fifth of scotch…Dyer held her above him as the thunder and lightning made their sex choppy… Hannah Beth crashed into her arms as her blond pigtails bobbled side to side.

Madison fell asleep dreaming of Hannah all night, seeing her over and over. She was very intimately drawn into the child's starry blue eyes, finally understanding their familiarity after all this time. When consoling Hannah's fears, watching her giggle, or listening to her stories, there had always been a sense that they had met.

Maladies always seem smaller in the light of a new day. Madison had clung to her routine, getting up and going to work if for nothing more than her own sanity. Again, she had reserved Dyer for her last appointment. She hadn't had the energy to face him any earlier. Dyer could be rationally relentless. Madison was sitting at her desk, wearing her reading glasses slightly low on her nose as she pretended to review his file. Dyer walked in talking on his cell phone. His childish sweet tone hinted he was talking to Hannah.

"I'm here with Mrs. Madison so I need to go honey – all right, but be quick."

Dyer handed the phone to Madison.

"Mrs. Madison it's Hannah Beth."

"Hello, my Hannah Beth. What are you up to?"

"I just got a new ladybug kite and I was wondering if you'd help me fly it when it gets windy again?"

"I'd love to help you. When did you start liking kites?"

"I always wanted one but Daddy said they might lift me off the ground and take me to China. Now that I'm six, I think I can handle it. Well, I gotta go. You gotta talk to Daddy. I don't want to get him in trouble."

"You take care, lady bug. We'll fly that kite together."

Madison's hands trembled ever so slightly as she carefully placed Dyer's phone on her desk. She silenced its ringer just as she had her urge to cry. She was trying to set the tone. The line between Madison and Dyer had been crossed, leaving it scuffed and ambiguous.

"The last time we spoke, you were going to finally clean out your wife's remaining clothes. Were you successful?"

"Hannah and I boxed them up and together took them to a shelter. Hannah was all right with it."

Madison put notes in his chart, feeling his chocolate stare burn a hole in her head. She knew this couldn't work; they couldn't be professional anymore.

"I slept with another woman."

"And how do you feel about that?"

Dyer watched her body, finding her unusually stiff and rigid.

"She's amazing, but I think she's avoiding me. She might be regretting it. I don't know much about her life."

"Maybe she is guarded in order to protect you? She might be very adept at that. She might not want you to see things about her that could compromise your relationship or your daughter?"

"Why would I need protection from her?"

"Her family is dangerous and association with her could have consequences."

"Madison, talk straight to me."

Madison stood and joined him on the couch. She caressed his knee. Everything softened. There was calm. They could both hear the wall clock's pendulum swinging back and forth.

Dyer brushed her long bangs out of her face. He removed her reading glasses, sliding them into his front shirt pocket. His curious gaze plumbed her soul.

"Rhett was an attorney for a mafia family in New Orleans. He worked with his uncle who married into it – it's just a long story."

"I'm listening."

"Rhett and his uncle stole money from the godfather of the family. Rhett helped him squirm around every legal hurdle, including murder accusations. We've done a lot of things I am not privy in speaking about. I am less than ideal."

Dyer rubbed his hands together, processing the sins of her husband. Her beautiful mouth made more sense. She knew keeping it tight would protect them.

"You know all about my life, yet you've never had the need to share yours. Why now? What are you not telling me?"

"If you get involved with me any further, you will be in danger. This family has had a lot of inner conflicts and power struggles over the years. Rhett's thick into his uncle's dirty dealings that made them a lot of money. His uncle intends to collect. He is circling Rhett, waiting for him to die. He will die. Vincent will guarantee it."

"I don't understand. What threat would I pose to him? I'm not an obstacle."

"I am now his uncle's direct route to everything they stole. If you get involved with me, you or Hannah could be the perceived obstacle."

Madison's lips were straight as the horizon line.

37

"That's just speculation."

"You can't ever make this equation equal. You and Hannah mean too much to me. I've never had a love like this. I couldn't live with myself if something happened to either one of you."

"You are in this alone, aren't you? That is why you can't quite push me away."

"You don't know what all is at stake."

"You are hiding things. You need me right now, but something is making you push me away. That's all right because I don't believe in making promises anymore. Nothing is free, Madison. I'll trust you, for now."

Dyer unbuttoned her top two buttons. Madison again watched his quick fingers. Dyer's hand disappeared under her skirt. Their sexual teamwork transcended the difficult words unspoken. She straddled him, lacing her fingers behind his neck. He grabbed Madison's thighs, lifting and laying her on her desk. Dyer's cell phone rang beside Madison's half-naked torso. He pushed it off the desk and into her trashcan. They tangled their bodies together, thrusting their doubt from skin to skin.

Hannah Brown

My name is Hannah Beth Brown.
My momma said I was named after my
great-grandma who was a fairy princess
ballerina and had an alligator as a pet. My
momma was always telling me silly stories.
I really got sad when she went to Heaven.
Now, I don't have a momma that can tell me
stories. Daddy tries to tell me bedtime
stories, but they are about houses and bricks
or boards and stuff. Daddy is happier now
that we go and see Mrs. Madison. She is
real good at listening. I can tell her anything
and she just smiles and writes it down on her
notepad. She tells me she is keeping my
words to whisper to Momma in Heaven one
day.

Daddy found my momma sleeping in
the bathroom and she wouldn't wake up. He
called the hospital and they took her to
Heaven. Daddy got really mad when
Momma left us for God.

I love coloring books. Mrs. Madison got me some new crayons. She is real good at staying in the lines. I got a kite that Mrs. Madison said she will help me fly. She knows all about strings and wind. Daddy says Mrs. Madison is a very special angel from Momma that is here to make us feel better when we miss her.

Daddy kisses Mrs. Madison on the lips like he did Momma. I wish Mrs. Madison could be my new momma. I asked Daddy if she could and he started telling me about those houses with bricks and boards and boring stuff. Mrs. Madison is a lot different than my momma. My momma had yellow hair and Mrs. Madison's is brown. My momma yelled and cried a lot and fought with Daddy. Mrs. Madison never yells or fights, but she does cry sometimes. She doesn't know I hear her in the bathroom before we talk. She is so pretty. Maybe one day, she can be my momma and we can all go live in that silly old house Daddy always tries to tell me about at bedtime.

I don't like Mrs. Madison's uncle. He talks to me some times after school before my daddy comes to get me. He has stinky breath. He's a big, fat guy who talks funny and tries to give me pistachio ice cream. He's nosy. My momma always said stay away from nosy people. I like getting ice cream with Mrs. Madison and Daddy. It is like having a family again.

Define Family

Rhett's eyes floated like bobbing corks in the river of his life. With lips so instinctively pursed, his cognition had been unable to process his emotional demons. Rhett's body seemed more languid. His silence transformed into lethargy. Madison had experienced this same intensely vivid behavior in her terminal patients.

Rhett hummed with his eyes closed, abruptly halting his off-key melody upon smelling Madison's perfume. He didn't talk to Madison, only conveyed strange glints of shame in his stare. She reached for his hand, but this time he grasped her fingers, kissing them. He brought them to his nose, smelling her skin. Her lotion was verbena and coconut. He had bought it for her years ago and she wore it in the summer months. He remembered the smells and tastes of their life together. Her skin and his had mingled into a woodsy jasmine-tasting sweet with a slightly bitter finish. Madison retracted her hand suspiciously.

45

"The kite I built. Don't ever give it away. It will be worth something one day."

He stared up at the muted television.

"He's going to kill me this time."

She walked to the door, making sure no one was around before closing it.

"Let me help you."

Rhett turned his back to her, curling his knees to his chest. Confrontations now sent him to the fetal position.

"I don't know what all these…things… are in my head. There's blood and dead bodies….People getting put into trunks…. and I'm holding a shovel…then, I see us at home together, normal…having coffee, reading the paper….I see my grandmother's Italian restaurant when I was a kid…smell her spaghetti….then I…hear voices…yours…mine...his….bad, bad words…sins."

Rhett's voice was muffled by his pillow as he spewed more syllables than he had since the accident. Madison rubbed his back in circular motions. Rhett rolled over to

46

her, wiping tears. Tears Madison had cried
a thousand times.

"Scary, isn't it?"

Rhett flung his weak hand in her
direction as if shooing a fly, frustrated by its
incessant buzzing.

"You....you just...just go
away...yeah...*just go away.*"

Rhett and Madison often found
themselves in heated arguments with Rhett's
uncle. Rhett used to kiss Madison's index
finger, telling her to *just go away.* Her reply
of understanding was *go where?* If he did
nothing, she left. If he rubbed her index
finger, she went to check his office safe.

"*Go where?*"

Rhett looked back up at the muted
television as he reached for the remote,
turning the volume to a low roar. The
weather man projected upper nineties and
killer humidity. He caressed Madison's
index finger.

Smoke and Mirrors

Rhett's law practice smelled of leather and cigars. Madison had closed his office, not returning since the day she found him. She felt like vomiting as the aroma slapped her in the face. Her transgressions closed in with condemnation, surrounding her like every wall of the room. She locked the door and old ghosts began chanting in a thousand different voices replaying old words.

The door to Rhett's office had been left open slightly in the EMT's haste. If she closed her eyes, she could hear him dealing, his voice smooth and wicked. Her life with Rhett cracked and popped through her with the flip of the light switch. The bloodstain was still on his desk and carpet – dark reddish black forever staining the ornate wood and cashmere rug. Rhett's desk was impeccably neat and tidy. Nothing was out of place other than the sporadic small splatters of blood. Madison sat in his chair, picking up a black and white photograph of them that was sitting on the front of his desk. Blood had sprayed across the glass onto their smiling faces. She felt small in Rhett's ill-fitted chair. It was formed to his body shape and weathered by his motions. It didn't squeak when she spun around. It was silent, smooth, and fluid.

Madison moved his chair and the rubber mat away to reveal a floor safe. She punched in a code and opened the heavy door. Inside their secret hiding place was a file containing Rhett's last will and testament updated and filed two weeks before his accident. She hurriedly scanned the document with her index finger. Rhett had left a parcel of rural woodlands in central Arkansas to….Madison. She had never wanted that land. Did not want any part of the carnage buried there. Money and property with a combined value at ten million dollars were left to…Madison. Huge tear drops mounted in her eyes, confirming Vincent's data…one million dollars put in a trust for Rhett's biological child given upon said child's twenty first

birthday….said child's name…Hannah
Brown. One million dirty dollars stolen by
Rhett and Vincent.

Things Lost or Stolen

Dyer had misplaced his cell phone.
His footsteps led him back to Madison's
office. His mind rewound their awkward
session just the day before. Their soul-
purging turned to sex, and he remembered
their syncopation working many things off
the desktop.

Snakes slither into cracks and
crevices we can't imagine they can fit
through. They sneak up on us at the most
inopportune times, when our guard is down
and no shovel is in sight. They make our
pulse race, our palms sweat, and our speech
incoherent or inaudible.

Dyer noticed the cigar smoke
instantly as he walked through the door.
Madison's high-back leather chair was
facing away from Dyer as a smoke trail
meandered like factory pollution above the

bald head seated there. Dyer paused, waiting for the smoke to speak.

"She ain't here, Mr. Brown."

The smoke stood. His cheeks sucked in and out furtively on the cigar, massaging the nicotine through his system as he examined Dyer. He offered his fat meaty hand. Dyer shook it.

"Vincent Bianchi. Rhett's uncle."

"I see Madison is out. I'll just come back later."

"Looking for this?"

Vincent reached in his pocket, pulling out Dyer's cell phone and handing it to him. Dyer's neck flushed a dark crimson.

"Might be a little more careful where you place your – stuff."

He chuckled at his own comment rather arrogantly, his big belly jiggling like Jell-O salad.

"What's your point?"

Vincent paced the floor back and forth, cracking his hairy knuckles as he prepared to lecture Dyer.

"You love Madison and I love Madison. You want her and I want her just for different - stuff."

"I'm no threat to your *stuff*."

"How long ya plannin' on sleepin' with Madison? 'Til *my* stuff's used up?"

"I don't want Madison's money."

"Right, 'cause it ain't hers, it's mine. She's going to give it to me and you're goin' to help, lover boy."

Vincent puckered his lips, kissing at Dyer. Dyer clenched his fists, his knuckles white.

"I'm not helping you."

Vincent reached into his expensive jacket. Dyer glimpsed Vincent's hand gun as he pulled out crumpled papers from his breast pocket.

"Let me know if you really *trust* her, Mr. Nine Months?"

Vincent threw the papers at Dyer's feet, flicking the ash from his cigar onto Dyer's boots and strutting to the door.

"Or maybe that's *thrust* her?

Vincent laugh was guttural as if the joke were on Dyer. Dyer already hated his smarminess. His high dollar clothing only housed walking garbage.

Vincent Bianchi

Late July 2007

I won't deny my family was rotten as fish heads. They killed any poor idiot that got in the way of money or power, even their own. They sent us my parents' bodies in trash bags for Christmas the year my sister and I moved in with our grandma. After the gunfire and bloodshed settled out, my sister kicked me and our family's heritage to the curb. I married a New Orleans bitch with connections.

Rhett was only a boy when he helped me load a guy into my trunk. The kid appreciated what a powerful motivator fear can be. We were all a good team swindlin' my father-in-law's fortune. Madison got good at turnin' a deaf ear. Rhett was always protectin' her pretty ass. When the money got too good, I got greedy and he got suspicious. My plan was runnin' along smoothly until Madison walked in. She's got bad timin', the lucky bastard. I almost had him cold.

Madison is loyal and is used to wipin' asses for a livin'. She wants to make things all better for her clients, includin' Rhett. I know Madison has access to everythin' Rhett hides. See, I am a gambler. I count on bad judgment. I have to make them doubt themselves or the other guys playin'. It makes it easier to spot weakness. Madison got a little too attached this time. What a sap. I could squash Dyer Brown like a cockroach. He thinks with his balls. A woman can send this kind of guy's reasonin' to the crapper. When you're in the crapper, you don't hear the toilet flushin', you just feel the water rushin' you down the pipe.

I just flushed the toilet on both their worlds today in the form of some info... each with their own puzzle piece. It was so easy a girl could have done it...matter of fact...a little girl did.

Along Came a Spider

Madison pulled into the drive, opening the garage door that creaked and popped like an old man with bad knees. She closed it immediately, shutting out the world, and it reverberated with a thud, hitting the concrete. Madison heard stifling silence for the first time since this nightmare had begun. The cool air from the cab was subtly overtaken by the new August humidity. Mosquitoes buzzed in her ears, looking for fresh blood. The dim light from the garage door windows cast long shadows across her as she sat frozen, clutching the wheel too firmly, lost in her own dilemma. Madison's yard needing mowing, the flowerbeds tending, her home more like a house abandoned awaiting a *For Sale* sign. She began crying, beating her hands on the steering wheel, frustrated by her own tears. Tears that now weighed one hundred pounds, dragging her down into her sadness and disappointment. She looked at her smudged makeup in the rearview mirror.

Her old life had crumbled. It was indicative in the fine lines under her eyes. She looked deceptively older, her hardened exterior housing something new.

Madison turned the weathered door knob, tiptoeing into the darkness. She turned on the standing lamp in the entryway and reached into her briefcase, pulling out the small device that swept for bugs. She cased the room, finally shutting it off, satisfied that no one was listening. Madison squelched the light again, dropping her briefcase. The light of the crescent moon illuminated her shadow as her silhouette faded in and out of the darkness. Her high heels clunked in unison as she kicked them from her feet into the middle of the living room. Low piano music began to emanate from the four corners. Ice cubes crackled as tequila sloshed into a crystal cut-glass. Madison floated to the window seat, a ghost amidst her former life. She watched the eerie stillness of dusk. The hot orange sun had fought the humidity before plummeting, an exiled mosquito fighting a thicket of patio netting. The only sounds heard were heavy fear in her rhythmic breaths and ice cubes rustling with every sip of liquor.

The choice to change his course, turn the wheel to the right rather than the left had led Dyer back to Madison's house. The bourbon had warmed his toes nicely, yet his control had begun to unravel. Dyer was a man of certainties. Each morning, he awoke, washed the sleep from his face, and slipped on his khaki pants. Barefooted and with precision, he walked his short drive to get the morning paper, knowing it took exactly twenty-three steps. Vincent's bombastic display of data and ill-repute had skewed Dyer's symmetry. He had replayed every interaction with Madison, searching for a reason not to trust her. He found nothing. Dyer's only certainty was the fact he meant nothing amidst this family theater. Yet, his beautiful daughter was tangled intricately in the mania.

Madison dropped her head back against the window facing when a brown spider began crawling her bare arm. Its tiny sly legs sent a rush through her body; her limbs jolted in unison. She swatted at the spider, shrieking just as Dyer approached her front door.

"Madison? Are you in there?"

Dyer dented her door, bruising his fist as he banged frantically. The door opened to darkness. Madison's lithe fingers clamped over Dyer's mouth, ripping his shirt sleeve as she pulled him through the door. Dyer couldn't see his hand in front of his face.

"Forget to pay your electric bill?"

Madison pushed Dyer away, disappearing like fog.

Dyer stumbled, pawing his way behind the scent of Madison's skin.

He slid beside Madison on the window seat, putting his arms around her. Madison smelled bourbon in his sighs. She tried to hide her sobs, holding her breath metrically in short spurts. Their closeness enunciated issues no listening device could capture. Misfortune caressed their divisive lives, smugly sending tiny ripples of doubt

through their hope. The elusiveness of
darkness is the only safe place souls can
commune.

"Who is Lane Godair to you?"

Dyer squeezed Madison closer,
shepherding her cooperation with his
questioning.

"She's a friend of ...the family."

Madison felt Dyer's cell phone
vibrating against her back. It had found its
way from her office drawer into his front
shirt pocket. She pulled away from him,
picking the phone from his pocket and
disappearing like a mist. Her bugging
device beeped loudly three times. She could
be heard fidgeting with the phone. The
toilet flushed. Dyer hadn't noticed
Madison's holster and gun strapped to her
outer thigh. Its authority brushed against
him in the unfamiliar darkness.

"Who is Lane Godair to *you*?"

Dyer cautiously ran his hand down
Madison's leg to the cold, steely gun,
removing it. He held it pointed toward the
floor as he kissed her earlobe.

"She's Hannah's birth mother."

Dyer held the gun with his left hand and searched his pant pocket with his right. His crumpled data about Hannah's biological mother would only reaffirm Madison's stoicism.

"You didn't know about Lane, did you?"

"No."

"I believe your uncle wanted me to share this with you, test our trust. I should have no reason to doubt you….right?"

Dyer felt Madison massaging his fingers that warily wrapped around her gun.

"I've been wearing a gun for *our* protection, not mine."

"Just give me that reason, Madison."

Vincent had planted the weed of suspicion in their relationship. Madison knew her answer would allow the weed to choke them.

"Hannah's birth father is Rhett."

Madison bled into the walls once again, returning with the data Vincent had given her. She folded it and slipped it in his front pants pocket.

"I think this was intended for you."

Dyer clutched his teeth and the gun simultaneously.

"How long…when did you know?"

"Yesterday."

Dyer's phone vibrated. It was Hannah.

"He knows you are here. Your phone was bugged. Where's Hannah?"

"She's safe."

Dyer fumbled, answering the phone.

"Hello, sweetie."

"Daddy, where are you?"

"I'm at Madison's. Honey, are you all right? Where's your sitter?"

"She put a big black spider in my closet again."

"You shouldn't go around saying such things."

Hannah's imagination had become her reality after her mother's death. Anxiety sent her inside that world.

"Let me talk to Mrs. Madison, please."

Hannah's tone was now anxious. He nodded at Madison, handing her the phone.

"Hannah Beth, talk to me."

"Can I come and stay with you tonight? I'm afraid the spider will come out of my closet again."

"Is it a make-believe spider or are you trying to tell me something?"

"He breathes heavy and has big black eyes that watch me."

"I understand. I won't let that spider get you."

"Hurry."

"Your daddy's coming."

They probed each other suspiciously, melding their shadows with the realization that they were merely two chess pieces in a wicked game.

Dyer throttled his diesel engine, waking the neighbors. As he drove away, he wrestled with thoughts of taking Hannah and getting lost, never to be found...leaving Madison alone and vulnerable. He would have done just that nine months ago. As he pulled into his own driveway, Dyer pulled Madison's gun out of the glove box, sliding it into the back of his belt.

Mafia Style

The tequila was smooth tonight, rewarding to her palate. She sat cross-legged in her window seat, cell phone ready to dial. She let the tequila push the button.

"It's Madison. Get on a plane... Yes, it is Vincent. You've all fucked me with a fine mess. I don't want excuses or reasons right now. Just materialize... Lane... I know about the baby."

Before leaving for Madison's house, Hannah slipped into Dyer's huge duffle bag he used for camping equipment. Her crystal blue eyes were all that were visible.

"Thanks, Daddy, for hiding me in your big bag. The spider can't find me here."

"Anytime, sweetie - now let's zip you up."

Dyer, lugging Hannah like camping gear onto his shoulder, used Madison's back door. He rapped three times then heard the deadbolt disengaging. The house was still dark as Dyer unzipped the laughing bag and dropped it on the couch.

Out of the darkness, tiny patters could be heard. Hannah ran into a table.

"Where are you guys?"

There was frustration in her sweet tone. Madison could smell the pure scent of Hannah's golden hair.

She wrapped her long arms around Hannah, holding her to her chest.

"What are you doing sitting in the dark?"

"We like the dark."

"You're crazy!"

Forgotten laughter echoed out of the thick sea of tension they were navigating. As Madison primped Hannah's pigtails, hindsight chipped away small flakes of ice around her heart.

"Mrs. Madison. Can I take a bath in your deep tub? I need to talk to you."

66

"Hannah Beth don't you take advantage of this situation. Mrs. Madison is being kind."

"It's girl stuff, Daddy."

Madison poured some of the lavender bubbles into the tub and the aroma wound through the blackness. Dyer remembered their first evening together in that tub. Madison's skin had smelled so clean and sexy.

Madison lifted Hannah over the tall tub wall and into the bubbles. She sank beneath them, staring at Madison with Rhett's blue eyes.

"What do you need to tell me, Hannah?"

"Daddy doesn't believe in spiders, does he?"

"Why do you think that?"

"He thinks I'm making it all up."

"We all pretend sometimes."

"*He's* not pretend."

"Does *he* scare you?"

"Nah…I just call you and he goes away."

The tip of Hannah's wet pigtails looked like sharpened pencils. She toweled off, insisting on wearing just a little bit of Madison's perfume.

"I wish you were my momma."

Hannah tried on a few bracelets Madison had left lying on the counter, twisting her wrists, examining the style in the mirror.

"You're my Hannah Beth. That is better than a daughter."

Hannah slept in the guest room. The bed was fluffy, secure and Madison's. Hannah asked Dyer to lie with her until she fell asleep. When he heard Hannah's breathing change gears, he closed the door, leaving her to dream of alligators and princess ballerinas.

Dyer heard Madison's shower running. He fumbled through a maze of furniture until her found her bedroom. The light of a lavender candle flickered wildly off the walls of her bathroom, giving shadows monstrous height. He stepped through the door, seeing Madison in the shower, her body almost dancing to the candle flame's rhythm.

Dyer unbuckled his belt, shedding his clothes. He joined her in the shower, watching the water course off her breasts. Dyer's breath met hers. His hands brushed her naked thighs. He kissed her back, moving into her, letting the pleasures of her skin numb his pain and frustration. Sex his sounding board.

Dyer increased the thrust of his hips, not noticing her body's stringency. He was taking his anger out on the betrayal of their trust. He finished, almost maliciously moving away from her. When he heard her bawling grow over the cadence of the powerful jet shower, he knew he had behaved no better than her uncle. He turned off the shower. Water rushed to a trickle. Dyer opened the shower door and reached for a towel, offering it to Madison's tears. It seemed they only cut the wound deeper with each move. Dyer didn't know how to touch her.

"What is wrong?"

"You asked me how I know Lane. Lane is Vincent's niece."

Dyer banged his hand on the shower wall. His eyes were deep, dark chocolate pools ruminating sadness.

"Your uncle has known this all along. He's playing us, don't you see?"

"This is what it is Dyer. We can't change it."

"You didn't know about Hannah, but you knew about the affair, didn't you?"

"It wasn't an affair."

Dyer rubbed the back of his neck, trying to make his love for her equal his rage.

"Oh...so you just used me...to get back at your husband...and at Hannah's expense."

"Everything I reveal pushes you away...You were always that one thing... that was mine and only mine."

Madison slapped him across the face. His unshaven cheeks highlighted the raw hurt that floated on the surface of his pores.

70

Hurt was ugly, contorting their behavior. The candle's war dance reflected wildly off their teary eyes. The candle had burned to the end of its wick. The flame dimmed to a smoke trail, leaving them in shadow.

Madison reached for his whiskers apologetically. Dyer took her hand and guided her to the bedroom. They intertwined in the safe arms of ambiguity without words or data, creating their own comfort. Their futures were fated by the welfare of a child that brought them closer, slowly tearing them apart.

In the Light of Day

The morning sun rays always awaken Dyer early. Madison's hair was tickling his face, taunting him just like her tears. He didn't move, watching Madison's body rise and fall, memorizing each breath and the feel of her body against him. She hid things that he'd never know. It was her nature, to shield others from her way of living. He

71

gathered Madison's mop of hair and brushed it aside, savoring the aroma of her skin before kissing her neck. Madison had cut him with information and actions she had not committed. Dyer had shot the messenger.

Dyer smelled Madison on his skin as he buttoned his jeans and closed the door. He left her sleeping hard, drool running out of her beautiful mouth. His naked toes tingled on the cold wooden floor with each step. He brewed a pot of coffee, remembering younger days when his life was fresh and unwritten. Before Lane Godair had befriended his wife and begged them to adopt her child. Dyer did the math and found a long line of coincidences that led him to Madison. Madison had just found out about Hannah and Rhett's shared biology, but she wasn't surprised about Lane. Madison was a horse of a different color, strong and firm, not bending to the desires of others. She was powerful and calculating. She knew how to firmly wear brass balls, competing like a man, never

72

letting her femininity be vulnerability –
except with Dyer. Dyer had abused that
openness with blame and selfishness.
When Dyer slanted things from Madison's
perspective, his perceived tragedy became
more of a "situation" she had to fix. It all
added up for the first time. His coffee
burned his tongue just as his insecurities
were now.

Dyer refilled his coffee, hearing the
birds chirp on her patio. He joined them,
admiring the breathtakingly steep view of
the Arkansas River. Madison's yard rolled
downward from lofty heights. The
oppressive heat of an Arkansas August was
upon them. The morning would begin with
an angry sun leering with its heat and the
southern humidity eventually making the hot
feel sticky.

Dyer had left the door open, the
screen door separating him from Hannah
and Madison. He heard Madison rustling in
the kitchen, her spoon bouncing from side to
side, stirring the cream and sugar in her
coffee cup. She joined him on the patio,

wrapping her arms around his waist and lacing her fingers with the precision of a zipper. He looked down at her hands and he felt her breasts on his back. Madison kissed the back of his neck, her lips still warm and soft from slumber. He turned, facing her and noticing sweat already forming on her upper lip and forehead. He studied her posturing for a long moment, trying to read her gestures. In daylight he could no longer hide his frustrations.

"Madison, last night...I'm sorry. Hannah and I...we have to leave."

"I know. Your hips are very adept at angry goodbyes."

"We can't tell you where we are going. You just...have to trust me."

"Damn you. You know I can't do that."

Madison bowed her head full of chestnut wavy hair, swiftly hiding tears.

"Then tell me what you know. Make me believe you."

She put her hands in the back pockets of his pants, pulling him close to her.

74

"It doesn't work like that. Don't you see? I can't tell you things. If I do...*you'll* die."

"Long before all this... madness ... I had made up my mind that I wanted you to be there for Hannah if something happened to me. I wanted you to be her legal guardian. I just knew you ...and your husband would give her a good home."

Dyer smirked, huffing at the irony. He pulled the papers from his pocket, handing them to her.

"After we got involved, I even imagined us raising Hannah together. Isn't that crazy?"

A box of Hannah's colored pencils lay strewn across the patio table. Madison reached for the dark green one and signed her name. She stuck the papers in the front of his pants.

"I don't think it's crazy at all."

Dyer caressed the back of her neck, kissing her softy over and over. The whiskers that had scraped and burned her skin the night before now tickled her mouth.

"I love you, Madison, but your life pisses me off. "

Madison ran her fingers through his hair, brushing the coarse temple cowlicks back into place.

"Hannah is a means to an end for Vincent. That is why you have to go and protect her like a pot of gold...because she is one."

Fork in the Road

Hannah had been pouting openly, clicking her seatbelt before Dyer asked her if she had buckled it. Dyer could tell something was off. He hadn't noticed Hannah hiding behind the patio door that morning, listening as he and Madison shared a very private conversation.

The humid August air wrapped them tightly, constraining them in their own clothing. Sweat grew like bacteria on their skin. Dyer blasted the air, drowning out the radio. He stomped his diesel as he pulled out of Madison's expensive driveway, just wanting to get the hell out of this mess. Dyer looked at Hannah in the rearview mirror. She sat in the center of his crew cab with her arms crossed in interrogation.

"Daddy, why are we leaving Mrs. Madison?"

"Mrs. Madison is no longer our counselor. We are fixed."

"I don't feel fixed."

"She wants us to move on, honey. That is why we are going to go away for awhile, together."

"Will we come back to Mrs. Madison?"

"I don't know. She will always be in your life. I promise."

"She signed papers to be my momma."

"Hannah Beth...You should not sneak around and be nosy. People close doors for reasons."

"But...the door was open. It was just the screen door...I just love her, Daddy. Don't you?"

Hannah stared back at Dyer in the rearview mirror, her blue eyes pleading. As they approached the interstate, Dyer took a fork in his usual path, pulling off at the hospital. He swallowed his pride, as it swam in his acidic stomach, realized the simple truths in Hannah's honest admission.

"Why are we here? Hospitals are full of scary people."

Dyer rapped his fingers on the steering wheel, searching for his own answer. He thought he'd just do a few errands and blow out of town. Madison's selective silence had born questions.

"I need to see someone before we leave."

Hannah held his hand firmly as they walked down the long corridor of rooms. She cut her eyes from door to door, looking at the people in their beds, some hooked up to machines or strange contraptions. Televisions blared from different rooms with each step. They found the hallway to Rhett's room.

A man guarded Rhett's door. He stopped them and made a phone call. Dyer clenched his teeth in anger, rubbing the back of his neck, knowing the man was speaking to Madison. He didn't have much time. The burly man got the OK and opened the door for them.

Rhett heard the door, was facing the window, looking out at the traffic. Monitors could be heard beeping and bed rest permeated the room. Rhett muted the television news channel, his stare dark and hollow. His mouth held a permanent scowl as he studied Dyer.

Rhett noticed the guard's broad shoulders through the window on the door. Madison still had him posted for protection, but had allowed their entrance. Rhett watched Dyer's hands massage Hannah's tiny shoulders. The pause between them was long and uncomfortable. Hannah fidgeted.

"I recognize you... from pictures. You're very good with your hands. You did

some work on some of my wife's...
stuff...Who are you little girl?"

Rhett looked down upon Hannah in
disgust. She moved beside Dyer, clinging to
his leg, unsure of this strange scary hospital
man.

"I'm Hannah Beth Brown."

Dyer's suspicions were confirmed as
Rhett's regretful fury elevated his breathing.
He squirmed in his decaying body. The
color faded from his already ashen skin,
giving him the look of death. Hannah
quickly stood behind Dyer, holding his leg
like a tree trunk.

"Guard - Get them out of here!"

Rhett's raspy voice raged. His chest
rose rapidly. His lips were pursed tightly as
his jaw clenched.

"Come to me Hannah Beth."

Hannah dropped her bag of coloring
books and the crayons fell to the floor,
scattering as she ran to Madison. Madison
held her for a long moment, absorbing her
tension, feeling her small body tremble. She
glared in disappointment at both men.

"I'm taking Hannah outside."

Dyer handed the bag to Madison and she snatched it, charging out the door with Hannah firmly in her grip. Rhett stared at the box of crayons Hannah had spilled in her haste then rather unemotionally stared back at the muted television. Dyer picked the crayons up one by one, putting them back in the box. Both men's anger floated on the surface of the gravity in the room.

Rhett reached into his bedside drawer, pulling out even more provocative pictures of Dyer and Madison. He had lined their movements sequentially, making them appear animated as he suckled the pain selfishly, letting it ruminate and consume him. He handed the pictures to Dyer, never taking his cold gaze off the news.

"Only a punk sticks his…*stuff* into things that aren't his."

Dyer threw the pictures back at Rhett and they scattered all over the floor, their steamy affair open for all to view. Rhett balled his frail fist.

"You found out about Hannah before the accident, didn't you? Vincent has known about her all along and that is why you told Madison. You are afraid of what he will do."

"I don't have to tell *you* anything…or explain why I did what I did."

"Hannah is more than a name on a piece of paper. She's my daughter with your DNA. I'm going to do my damndest to protect her from your family."

Rhett banged his fist on the mattress.

"You don't understand *my* family."

Dyer grabbed Rhett's fist, leaning over him.

"I may be a simple man, but I am smart enough to figure out things your wife hides for you."

"She's just screwing you."

"You shouldn't give me a lecture about sticking *my stuff* into things that aren't mine. Madison was more than turn about, and that is what pisses you off. If something happens to me, I have nothing to lose. Madison is Hannah's legal guardian. I just gave her what she always wanted – your child."

Dyer released Rhett's small fist. He picked up the racy photographs, flipping through them before setting them on Rhett's chest that labored in anger.

"My marriage is none of your goddamn business."

"That little piece of your DNA on a piece of paper that you wrote off is my beautiful baby girl. That makes it my business, too. You and I…we are family."

Hannah bounded through the door, searching for her box of crayons. Dyer had placed them on the bed by Rhett's legs. Hannah apprehensively approached the crayon box.

"Looking for these?"

Rhett handed them to Hannah with a smile.

"I'm sorry if I yelled at you."

"It's OK. I understand. You're just sick and hospitals make people weird."

"You're a very smart girl."

"Nah, Mrs. Madison explained it all to me."

Dyer took Hannah's hand, leading Rhett's DNA out the door and into a family tie that would change her tiny world no matter how hard Dyer Brown tried to shield it.

Heartbreak Warfare

Madison cornered Dyer as he barreled out of Rhett's room like a bullet. Dyer couldn't fight her because Hannah was in tow. Madison rumpled his shirt as she pulled him aside.

"Hannah, go over to that vending machine and get us a candy bar."

Dyer reached into his pocket, pulling out a few dollars, and giving them to Hannah. She cautiously left them within earshot, very aware of the verbal bombs exploding all around her.

"What were your intentions bringing Hannah here?"

"She's more than a name and now he has a face to never forget."

Madison put her face in her hands, growling.

"So you were gloating, rubbing it in?"

"You didn't stop me when the guard called you, did you? There's a part of you that wanted me to do what I just did."

"What *did* you do?"

"I just called it like I saw it."

"And how do you see it?"

"I wanted him to see all he is about to lose, real people, not names on paper. I want him to suffer the consequences. "

"His family doesn't work like that."

"Fuck his family and his paper people and money."

"You of all people know that life isn't fair."

"But it always equals up in the end, no matter how much it seems to lean one way or the other. It *is* that simple, Madison."

Hannah brought Dyer a Butterfinger. She handed it to him with tears in her eyes.

"Please don't fight."

Hannah put an arm around Madison's leg and one around Dyer's, pulling them close. Dyer's hand found Madison's and he pulled her toward him with Hannah sandwiched in the middle.

"Give me a hug, Mrs. Madison."

"Come here, my Hannah Beth. I want more than a hug."

Madison bent down to Hannah, wrapping her arms around her tiny frame as she kissed each cheek and eventually her button mouth.

"Remember what we talked about. You don't ever have to be afraid. You tell your daddy about the real spider if you see it. He will protect you."

"Thanks for being my new momma."

"I'm always here for you and your daddy. I will always be whatever you want and need."

Dyer fought the tears in his eyes. Madison had been everything the two of them had needed in the nine months since his wife's death.

"Hannah left a few things at your house. We have to pick them up and we'll be going."

"Kiss her goodbye, Daddy."

Dyer and Madison both grinned through their anguish, appeasing Hannah's fantasies. The realization that Madison might never see either one of them again sent ripples of anxiety through her body. Dyer felt it in her quaking touch. They kissed softly on the lips, leaving their words of regret tasted and unspoken. Madison released her fingers that had been laced zealously in his, sending them back into the unknown.

Hannah and Dyer found his truck in the busy parking lot. It looked like a gang of pigeons had defecated all over the hood and windshield.

"Ew! Bird poop!"

Hannah shrieked as she carefully avoided the crusted poop on her door handle.

On the ground were remnants of popcorn and a cigar butt. As Dyer opened the door, he noticed a flyer stuck to his windshield. It was an advertisement for a car wash. On the back, a handwritten note read - *It is going down tonight, punk* - clever sabotage by hungry pigeons. He crumpled the note and threw it in the parking lot by Vincent's cigar butt.

Death Wish

Something was different as Madison opened the door to Rhett's room. The air was stagnant and still. Rhett's energy saturated the walls. It was an energy Madison dreaded, full of dusty, dark karma that schlepped upon her, thick as an unwanted touch.

Rhett turned the television off. He threw the tawdry pictures of Madison and Dyer's intimacy up into the air like confetti and began clapping his hands slowly at first, then faster to the rhythm of his frustration.

Rhett's stare pierced Madison, inciting a learned guilt he had conditioned.

"Bravo! The camera liked your performance. You two are very photogenic."

Madison put her hands over her face, shielding her tired soul from his pull and push. Rhett's narcissism had been heightened with the accident. He was like reasoning with a brick wall. He grabbed a picture that had landed on his leg, sticking it in place of his own face, his eyes sarcastically peering over the top.

"I have to ask. Was it worth it…the sex for their lives? You know they are now good as dead."

Madison picked up one of the pictures from the floor, studying it for a long moment. Dyer was holding Madison from behind, kissing the nape of her neck very tenderly as she rested against him. His strong arms shielded her nakedness from the camera and the world. She turned the picture to Rhett, hugging it against her chest.

"Why did you keep these pictures, study them?"

"Don't try to counsel me…"

"You know it in your heart. It wasn't just sex. Look at how he touched me. It is obvious we were making love."

Rhett ripped one of the pictures into unrecognizable bits. His red face sulked. He swung at Madison and she caught his feeble punch.

"What? Did I hurt *your* feelings? Damn me to hell for actually having some of my own."

Madison squeezed his fist until he flinched. The room suffocated them with death and foreboding.

"I gave you *everything* in the will and this is how you repay the family?"

"Everything is just your lustful screw ups with strings attached."

"Lane was just a piece of ass and part of Vincent's grand plan. The child – consider it a gift."

Madison slapped Rhett across his smooth cheek, leaving the force of her rage in the form of her red finger imprints. Death's proximity purged their souls' emotional attics of all the hoarded garbage until there was nothing left - only pure truth.

"They are *everything* to me."

"So it's love. When I'm cold, you'll go off with the carpenter and play house?"

Madison didn't reply. Rhett's mouth curled with pride. He laughed wickedly, clapping his hands as Madison fumed in disgust. He thought he knew the woman he had mastered and manipulated.

Madison brushed the remnants of his curly blonde hair over his ear, stroking his temple where the bullet's exit left a scar. There was something maternal in her touch Rhett had never fathomed to observe. It complemented her demeanor, softened her edges, making him even more jealous of her.

"Oh, I've fallen in love again...with that little - gift - you left me."

Dead Bolts

Hannah had insisted on packing her toys and clothes, running Dyer into another part of Madison's house. She skulked,

91

delaying their departure. As Hannah packed her backpack, her eyes kept finding a door down the hallway Madison had kept closed. Hannah tiptoed to the forbidden room. She jiggled the knob, noticing it wasn't locked. Her curiosity imagined other worlds behind the fluid hinges. Alligators and princess ballerinas slithered and twirled in secret. The waning daylight beamed through the skylight, giving the hanging kites in the room the magical illusion of flight.

Dyer heard Hannah sigh in wonder. He watched her from around the corner but didn't stop her. He let curiosity guide the passions she shared with her biology. Hannah was frozen, fancying the kites with *oh* and *ah* as her eyes cased the room's grandeur. She moved over to a desk filled with kite strings, tools, and wispy, colorful kite tails. Dyer's heart sunk. He had hoped that bending her with his simple upbringing would render her immune to the very desires and pleasures that seemed to now be hard wired. Hannah brushed the strewn kite gadgets out of her way. The object of her affection sat on the back of the table. It was a black and white framed photo of Madison laughing very candidly, her arms crossed. Hannah stroked the photo with her index finger before sliding it into her backpack, stealing Madison's smile for the gray days ahead.

Keys unlocking doors can incite fear reminiscent of the jailer locking a prison door. The key unlocking the deadbolt alarmed Dyer. He walked toward the noise as the door slowly swung open, the intruder startled by the shuffle of other people. Dark, curly hair and a large brown eye peered around the door frame.

"It's you. What are you doing here? Where's Madison? "

Lane had cleared her clientele, boarding a plane as soon as Madison called.

"Don't worry. We're leaving as soon as she gets her things together."

"What? She's leaving with *you*? Why? Rhett isn't even dead."

Lane moved through the door, unable to control the panic in her inflection.

Dyer smiled as Lane pursed her lips in shock.

"I'm referring to my daughter who is gathering her stuff in the other room. Madison has been good to us. Thanks for recommending her counsel."

Dyer watched Lane put two and two together, her eyes bulging in fear.

"You and Madison…this is some kind of *sick* coincidence. I *won't* do this right now."

Lane turned to leave and Dyer grabbed her arm. He had forgotten how dramatic she could be.

Dyer noticed the red key on Lane's keychain she rubbed over and over with her thumb.

"Do all your family members have a key to Madison's home?"

Dyer reached in his shirt pocket, pulling out one of the photos Rhett had given him along with a copy of the papers Madison had signed. He handed them to Lane smugly. She turned the photo horizontally then vertically, furious at their

94

execution of intimacy, finally flipping to the signed document. Dyer felt a strange tinge of jealousy from her. She folded the paper and slipped the photo back into his pocket, patting his prominent peck.

"Sex doesn't constitute family. Good luck with that."

"In your case it did."

"You're both just incidentals I have to work around."

Lane crossed her arms, posturing defensively. Dyer noticed how Lane and Hannah had like self-protective structures. Dealing with Lane was like parenting his daughter.

"That incidental is only six. She is through teething and doesn't bite. She is just a little girl… even if she is the spawn of two devils."

"Madison called *me* to help her with this!"

Lane raised her voice. Her Cajun accent echoed dogmatically off the hardwood floors.

"Help her this time rather than betraying her."

"I've changed... People can change."

"Not really. They just get better at hiding their secrets."

Lane's coal black eyes that had just cut him coldly were now gray with shame.

"I don't know if I *can* do this."

"One day when she's older, Hannah will find you. What then?"

When Hannah heard a female voice she anticipated Madison. She came bounding around the corner with her backpack in tow. Her curled smile fell when her eyes met Lane's. Lane's and Hannah's body language was parallel. Hannah ran to Dyer. Lane kept her arms crossed. Her brown eyes as suspicious as Hannah's starry blue ones.

"Daddy, why are you yelling?"

"We're not yelling, honey. We're discussing something."

"You've sure been yelling a lot of it."

Hannah crossed her arms. Lane cheered on the child's blatant honesty with a chuckle. Lane and Hannah shared a smirk of agreement.

"I'm Lane, Madison's lawyer."

"I'm Hannah Beth. She's my momma."

"Madison is a very…lucky lady."

Denial had an awkward pause that buzzed in the echo of Hannah's words. Lane's regret clung, mere particles of dust suspended momentarily, never consciously acknowledged, absorbed into the room.

"It's time to go. Lane has a lot to work on."

Dyer loaded Hannah into his truck with her bags. Lane rummaged through Madison's refrigerator, finding a half-empty bottle of chardonnay. She pulled the cork off, turning the bottle skyward as her tears raced gravity. Dyer's diesel engine whined down the street toward the distant horizon. Hannah pulled the photo of Madison from her backpack.

.

To Masks and Family Ties

Lane heard the garage door open, the car engine purred for a long minute before shutting down. The door from the garage pivoted slowly, piercing the darkness. High heels could be heard, ceasing abruptly with a thump. Lane was lying on the couch as despondent soft sobs grew. Lane flipped on the lamp beside the couch, looking for the crier. Madison sat barefoot in the doorway. She had kicked off her expensive shoes, sliding onto the floor and pulling her knees to her chest. Madison's face was now buried in her crossed arms. Her very private sorrow echoed melodiously, searing Lane's guilt. Lane shut out the light and began crawling toward the haunting tune. She blindly pawed for Madison, catching her foot and following it up the leg attached. Lane rested her hands on Madison's clutched fingers. For a brief moment there was nothing but silence, sheer vulnerability between them.

"Rhett just died."

"I'm... sorry."

Madison raised her head, their breaths upon the other in the shadows. Madison could smell her distinctly expensive wine in Lane's exhale. She slapped Lane across the face, shoving her into the gloom and onto her back.

"No, you're not."

Lane moved slowly, rubbing her throbbing cheekbone. She stroked Madison's knuckles with her index finger.

"I took care of the money situation. That should buy you some time with Vincent...until you find Rhett's will."

Madison morphed into a shadow, slipping through the dimly lit evening. On the counter, she noticed the silhouette of the wine in question, the bottle now empty. Madison handled the empty bottle roughly, projecting her fury onto the neck, squeezing it sporadically.

Lane's fingers brushed against Madison. The two women were face to face, profiled by the street lights shining through the kitchen's large windows.

Lane's skinny fingers probed Madison's inner thigh. She found the revolver, pulled it out of its holster, removed the clip, and placed it on the counter.

Madison opened the refrigerator, pulling out another bottle of expensive wine. She handed it to Lane.

"Go ahead. Enjoy it like everything else of mine."

Madison pivoted toward the bedroom and Lane grabbed her wrist, desperately trying to stop her. Madison's body was rigid and unforgiving. Lane loosened her grip, bowing her head and surrendering to Madison's rage. Madison's footsteps resounded as she disappeared, slamming the bedroom door.

Lane Godair

I don't know how I got here. It seems with each move I make I find myself further and further away from the truth. I won't lie. I wanted my money over principals in the beginning of this family drama. Vincent blackmailed me with a dirty family secret that threatened my inheritance. I gave up my body and soul my last year of law school. I stayed the summer with the Peacock's, working as Rhett's intern. Rhett and Vincent played emotional ping pong and I was the ball. They manipulated me right out of my family's favor.

Madison tried to save me many times. I was so mired in my family's sludge that I couldn't see clearly. Soon, we were both immersed in their cycles of chaos and cover-up. When the summer was over, I thought I had escaped with some reprieve. I found out I was pregnant. Dyer's wife sealed my fate, pleading to adopt my baby, tangling Dyer and Hannah in my bed sheets.

Madison and I have a connection rooted in horrific terrors. We can never fully hate each other because, despite animosities, we need the other to rectify Vincent. I am considered difficult and emotionally void. Frigidness is the only thing keeping me together. If I give into the warmth of anyone, I will melt and fall to pieces. Madison can only see the darkness I wear as a wall. It is my own fault. I never let her see the changes she instilled. The gaze in Madison's eyes tonight almost makes me cry.

Out With the Old

Death stirs the living. Flies
incessantly buzz around a new carcass,
waiting to get their turn feeding off the
sadness and misfortune of others. Mornings
had always refreshed Madison's mindset.
The day of Rhett's funeral was a humid
August morning, the most oppressive day of
the year. As she zipped the back of her
dress, her eyes wandered toward Rhett's
closet. She entered, flipping on the light.
Inside were rows of suits. There was no
warmth to him as she shuffled through the
platitudes. Crisp white shirts, shiny wingtip
shoes, even his casual clothes were semi-
dressy, button down polo shirts, his jeans
designer, his tennis shoes over one hundred
dollars a pair. Finally, in the back of the
closet she noticed the light blue hue - his
favorite t-shirt. It read *go fly a kite* and on
the back was a large kite whipping in the
wind. It was threadbare and soft. She had
hated how he coveted it. She threw it onto

the bed as Lane sipped coffee, watching from the doorway.

Lane had floated on the periphery of Madison's anger, never quite stepping into it. They had been civil, all business. The air around them was loaded with unaddressed stagnancy.

Madison's clean, freshly bathed scent hit Lane in the face. Madison had chosen a chocolate sundress, black was for mourners. Lane admired her sinewy curves, hoping Rhett was fuming in hell. Madison fought with her earrings. Frustration shadowed her weariness. She threw the pearls on the bed beside Rhett's t-shirt, her fingers trembling horribly.

"Here, let me do that."

Lane moved behind her, locking the pearls into place. Lane's hands were shaking, too. She patted Madison's shoulders, her touch lingering.

"What do you need to tell me, Lane?"

"Vincent is close."

The Funeral

The funeral was at ten-thirty in the morning, the August weather too thick for an afternoon graveside. Rhett's family would not be attending. There wasn't bad blood between them, just no blood at all, no connection. Non-stories abounded when Madison thought of her extended, now expired family. Rhett had cut them out of his existence. He had been dead to them a long time, the shadow of a son whispered about in certain circles. There were no more than thirty people that arrived. Everyone met around the hearse at the funeral home as they prepared to follow to the cemetery. There was no service, only the burial. All the attendees lined up and followed Rhett's casket just the way he had planned it.

Lane sat beside Madison. The expression on their faces during the burial could have been mistaken as sorrow. Madison placed a red rose on Rhett's coffin. No one spoke after the service and there wasn't much interaction as most left immediately in hushed whispers. Madison thought she had smelled Cuban cigar smoke distantly in the southern breeze.

The Red Key

The two weeks after Rhett's burial had been brutally hot and humid. Madison had been sweeping her dirty life into nice piles. Lane had been very suspiciously accommodating. Vincent's cigar smoke lingered.

This mid-August morning was unseasonably cool. Cold fronts rarely slice the humidity this time of year. Strong, dark coffee brewed as Madison walked down the empty hallway. She sat in the window seat, one leg curled under her as the coffee shook the sleep from her foggy eyes, rousing her lucidness.

Madison opened the window, catching winds from other latitudes. They washed over her face with earthy, fresh scents. The unusually ample rainfall had left this summer dawn renewed.

Madison reached in her robe pocket, pulling out the shiny red key Lane had delivered just days prior to Rhett's death. She could almost hear seagulls crying overhead and waves licking at her toes as the salty air curled her hair.

She stared at the boxes stacked under the storage building's awning. The red key unlocked her new door.

Section II

Beach Music
Late August 2007

Dyer noticed the change immediately as he rounded the corner of Madison's street. The *For Sale* sign in bright red and blue caught his eye. He and Hannah had just returned from two weeks of being followed by Vincent. Dyer had been worried when he found Hannah in his large duffle bag, complaining of the spider on more than one occasion. Dyer knew the spider was real because Hannah was even reluctant to go to her favorite places, always watching over her shoulder.

Dyer knocked and his heart accelerated to his fist's pounding as the door opened to emptiness. Madison's home was now a series of boxes strategically placed for specific purposes or uses. Her former life now organized into a series of keepsakes and trash. It consumed Dyer that it had only taken two weeks to pack up everything and put it up for sale. His face was somber as his eyes chased the vacant corners. She

111

stopped stacking boxes and admired the gray around his temples. It complimented his pensive brow.

"I wasn't expecting *this*."

"I've wanted *this* for a long time, Dyer."

Dyer rubbed the back of his neck, looking down at Madison's beautiful hardwood floors now dusty and dirty from the shuffle of people. Madison felt Dyer staring a hole in back of her head as she tossed the remaining things into the box. Men don't cry often. Dyer was no exception, but tears can fall without falling. His eyes wept while remaining dry.

"Can't you see me for the woman I really am?"

Dyer paced, running his hands over his face in frustration. He reached for Madison's cheek, wiping her smeared mascara that had dried from previous tears. He kissed Madison, hungry and open-mouthed. She felt his fear, his lack of control working in syncopation with her own. She now understood how they had fallen into each other. She put her forearm between them, holding her feelings at bay.

"I'm just tired of hurting you and everything I touch. You and Hannah…us…*this*…It's that one thing in my life that is real."

"*This*…it will always be for Hannah. I do see you. I've always seen you for who you really are, Madison. You just can't and you won't let me show you."

The front door crept open and one starry blue eye peered around the door. It was Hannah.

"Daddy, did you forget me?"

"Never, Hannah Beth."

Hannah ran toward Dyer and Madison, wrapping her little arms around Madison's long legs.

"I've missed you, sweet pea."

Hannah noticed the empty house and boxes. She squeezed Madison tighter. Madison stroked her ponytail.

"Are you leaving us?"

"I'm moving. I am never leaving you. I promise. I'll be back."

113

"You will forget me."

Hannah poked Madison with her tiny pink fingernail, crossing her arms as she lowered her chin.

Madison knelt, lifting Hannah's apple-shaped face with her index finger. Their teary blue eyes were level.

"Let me make one thing very clear, Hannah Beth Brown. I will never leave you or forget you."

Hannah's beautiful lips curled in understanding.

"Good…cause, I love you… Momma."

Madison pulled Hannah into her chest, rocking back and forth, quelling her own dread. Dyer sighed, his hands in his front jean pockets. Madison winked at him.

"I've just got to go swat a few more spiders."

Life is a Highway

Madison went to Rhett's storage and retrieved his red antique Cobra convertible, gassed it up, and popped the top, heading south to the Gulf Coast. Rhett had bought the Cobra at a car auction because it was Madison's favorite antique. He had always taken incredible care of the car, driving it often and maintaining it perfectly, like his kites.

Her destination was her new beach home in Gulf Shores, Alabama. It was a few miles from historic Fort Morgan. Madison had just entered Jackson, Mississippi, as the heat of August sweltered. Her cell phone rang. Madison put the caller on speaker phone to navigate the exit.

"Your lover is a fuckin' punk. He tore up my best boy's arm. It's fractured like his skull's gonna be. I was just playin' with him."

"I think that is called...stalking."

"I've been chattin' with Lane. She's been real helpful. So, you're goin' away. Don't be spending that time on *my* money."

"I just buried my husband. There is nothing new to report."

Madison made a quick right.

Vincent breathed heavier, agitated.

"So cold... No love for Uncle Vincent? Consider Rhett's death a favor. I expect one in return... this could have been *much* worse."

"Did you say *worse*? My family is *dead*...my life is an etch-a-sketch."

"Did you know little girl's necks snap like toothpicks? The cartilage is like bubble gum."

Madison hung up, throwing her cell phone into the floor. She found his logic narcissistic. Murder wasn't a life vest just as terrorists didn't receive a medal of honor. Vincent had a way of making an antique car feel like a jalopy. She made the turn taking her further south, closer to freedom from the verbiage of emotional manipulators. She could almost smell the ocean.

Stranded

Water is for sailors, but the sky is for dreamers. Rhett had whispered that in

116

Madison's ear as she had gotten her first view of the ocean. They had been dating and slipped away for a long weekend together one hot September. The rush of the vacation season was subsiding and leveling out and they found a private, secluded beach house similar to this one. She missed that sort of innocent simplicity as she pulled into the sandy drive, the convertible sliding into place. She stood, stretching her legs after the long drive, inhaling the fresh breeze coming from the Gulf; winds from other dreamers.

Madison took off her shoes, feeling the cool sand work its way between her toes. She rolled up her jeans and headed in the direction of the boardwalk with Rhett's favorite kite. The sun was a hazy, angry orange as it set, leaving octopus-like tentacles wildly flailing in its fury. *There is always a breeze on the water; a kite master's dream.* Madison took Rhett's kite and began running down the beach as it ascended erratically at first, fighting the force of the wind but finally leveling out, working with Mother Nature's power. Rhett had never flown this one, had made it his masterpiece. She had kept it as he requested. But, it had too much potential to sit idly on a shelf. Madison felt Rhett pumping through her heart, could hear him cheering her on as the kite danced with the orange octopus in the sky. Madison stopped, turning to watch the kite float, her warm tears wiped with the ocean breeze. She screamed in joy and anger at the kite's dance.

"You son of a bitch - Look at her go!!"

Madison jumped up and down, marveling in what Rhett had created and had always promised was his best. Madison had always wished he had put as much into their life together as he had everything else. The kite crashed into the rigid sand, splintering. Madison dropped the strings, falling to her knees. Kite strings – that is all she ever was to Rhett. As Madison grieved for Rhett in long, labored sobs, a lone beachcomber admired her very public display from afar.

The beach house was modest and simplistic in décor. There was an old soaker tub with claw feet. It invited Madison with its smooth porcelain texture. She had stopped at a nearby grocery, picking up a few necessities and realized she had been buying for one person for years. Rhett always ate out with clientele. She poured a glass of chardonnay and eased into the tub filled with lavender scents. Madison was stranded, alone with only her demons - thoughts so powerful, motivating her to depths of anger, grief, fear, and redemption. It was time to let go in the privacy of the ocean air. She raised the window slightly as the blue-gray hues of vesper beamed down upon her nakedness. The ocean's rhythmic tides slowed her blood, soothed her mania. She spread the bubbles around her breasts and shoulders, finding her body rigid and taunt, hoping the hot water could loosen her muscles and her inhibitions. She was wound too tightly, a clock on the verge of springing apart wildly. Madison closed her eyes, slipping down deeper up to her neck, letting the bubbles tickle her nose and lips.

In that place between wake and sleep where we dump our fantasies or do mental gymnastics, erotic flashes of her romances popped like bubbles in a frenzy; lying naked in Rhett's arms, wrapped in a blanket on the beach at dusk; lightning snapping branches and throwing them against her bedroom window as she hovered above Dyer, kissing him deeply, revealing herself intimately to a mere stranger. Madison finished her wine in one gulp, throwing the glass against the wall, smashing it into pieces. *Damn them all.*

Moonlight silhouetted Madison's skin as sleep eluded her. She lie wrapped in the cotton bed sheet, the ocean air thick, pulling old memories from pockets of her psyche that had been locked tightly and purposefully. Her body ached; heartache physically hurt. She wanted no one. What she wanted was closure. Closure was what all her patients wanted from the beginning, the elusive goal that seemed to hide the harder you reached for it. To them, closure meant the end of the incessant ache. Madison now understood their plight. Ache had befriended her. Her grief would be prolonged with the settling of the will.

She wrapped her naked body in the sheet and retrieved her half-empty bottle of wine. Madison went upstairs to the attic room. The moon was full as she opened the window. The room's colors were vintage seventies, reminding her of her childhood, untouched throughout the years. The moon was so close she could almost introduce herself. In its abstract craters, she saw faces from her life. Deep into the midnight hour, Madison lined up her choices, connecting the dots to the very spot where she now found herself. The counselor inbred into her subconscious knew where her troubles originated – her father-figure. Madison had never known her own father. With Rhett, love seemed conditional, something she had to earn. Madison took off the sheet; the humid August air blanketed her in sweat. The back of her neck was soaked. She pulled her thick hair up with her hands, holding it off her neck. She felt Rhett oozing out of her pores as she worked him out of her system with the wine. Soon the perspiration turned to tears as Madison sobbed, pleading with the moon to take Rhett's biology out of Hannah. It had been the invisible knife in her chest. She wanted to tidy up their disastrous marriage and forgive herself. As she wiped tears, she caught a glimpse of her moonlit face reflected in the open window. At first, it startled her. Madison hadn't recognized the angst in her own eyes.

Madison awoke lying on her side, naked and cradling an empty wine bottle like a baby between her breasts, wishing it were Hannah. She opened her eyes to the soft light of a new day, cutting her body into sections of light and dark, the story of her night. The aching was gone, her heart lighter, her head fatter. She threw the bottle to the floor, the odor now nauseating. It had been her best and only friend last night.

She skipped coffee, needing air. Madison took a beach walk. There were few beachgoers out so early in the morning and so late in the season. Most were homeowners enjoying the end of the season or tidying up after the rush of families. The tide was high and volatile as storm clouds brewed in the distance. The gray water and sky accented the white caps of the angry ocean, making the scenery different shades of monotone. The world seemed softer, less vivid to Madison. The sand challenged her balance, working leg muscles not often used on the pavement. Her breathing accelerated and she could smell the wine from last night in her perspiration. The scent sickened her, made her stop and sit on someone's boardwalk steps, putting her head between her knees. A voice from the other end of the boardwalk called out to her.

"Are you all right?"

A tall, lean man walked over to Madison, standing above her. He was wearing running shorts and shoes, his body bronze, almost leather from the sun – the contrast making his salt and pepper cropped hair louder.

"Hangover."

Madison looked up to him and he smiled, seeing she was beautifully green.

"Oh."

"Bought that house…just got here last night."

Madison's voice was soft, subdued from the wrenching of her gut as she pointed to her new abode. She jumped up, running to the ocean to vomit. The man followed her. She turned, staggering into him and he walked her back to the boardwalk.

"Damn wine."

She looked to him, not at all embarrassed at her erratic display. Madison had an attraction to confession and complete strangers. They didn't judge or condemn.

"Madison."

She extended her hand in thanks.

"Houston."

He shook her hand, noticing her long slender fingers. She had been the kite flyer with the abandon he had admired.

Life in the Fast Lane

The ceiling fan creaked in a rhythm that was hypnotic. Madison had returned to the beach house, sleeping until early afternoon. Her cell phone rang on the nightstand and she found its chime complimentary to the fan's sedating whirl. She was in a state of flux, unaware of her surroundings, looking for Rhett – no, Dyer – time and space were overlapping – her parallel lines crossing over one another. Neighboring children laughed and shrieked in pleasure. Her mind drifted to Hannah and how she would love the ocean and sand. Madison rolled over slowly, hearing the ocean waves as the sunlight warmed her body. The perimeter of the room was cold and empty.

The cell phone beeped Lane's missed call, signaling voicemail.

"I hope you are enjoying the silence although I don't know how you can after total chaos. We need to talk…about things. Call me when you're sober. "

Things were vague, yet implicit. In very uncomfortable silences between the two there was an unspoken communication. Their shared experiences had created the connection. It was real, transcending the tragedy and betrayal.

Madison and Lane had gotten close that summer Lane worked for Rhett. Lane had a lot of personal issues she confided to Madison. Madison had chalked up Lane's oddities to her upbringing. Lane's family was an anomaly.

Lane threw her phone onto her desk in frustration after leaving Madison the voicemail. She stomped across her office and was almost out the door when her phone rang.

"What."

Madison sounded muffled as she lay on her side under the covers, her face half buried in the pillow.

"Well, hello to you, too."

"Keep it short. I'm not in the mood."

"Hang over?"

"Quit being a bitch."

"When do you want me there?"

"Umm...."

"Madison... when?"

"Next week. I need some time alone."

Lane hung up the phone, throwing it across her office. She knew Madison was stalling. Madison's weary fingers dropped her phone onto the floor. Both women cradled volatile emotions like crystal.

Madison walked out onto the deck and into the balmy afternoon heat. She watched the children dance across the sand, giggling. A young couple walked, holding hands along the shoreline. In the distance, she noticed the man from the morning who had helped her on the beach. He was running. He looked in Madison's direction. Houston smiled, his teeth glowing white against his tan skin. She watched him until he disappeared, a ghost into the haze.

The Broken Kite

The kite looked like a wounded bird, its tail flailing behind it in pain as it lay on the porch. Madison had brought Rhett's kite repair kit. It was elaborate with new parts for any kind of kite skeleton. She flipped it open, looking for a new *thingy* for the one she had broken. The sunset breeze began to pick up, cooling the sweat on her forehead. She worked her nimble fingers, fixing the broken part, reinforcing it where it was now weak, vulnerable. She understood the mind-numbing effects of building and letting go. She felt close to Rhett, thumbing through his kit and fixing his kite. The sound of the waves and the warm sunshine strengthened her in her own broken places. Fixing the kite was part of her grief.

It was time for a test run. The wind was volatile. She began moving backward down the beach, looking at the kite as it fought its way into the sky. It twisted a few times and she feared it might break in the same place, but it held firm, leveled out and danced for her, fighting her angrily. Madison pulled the kite strings back, giving it more play, pulling it back again, crying the whole flight. When the evening turned dark and her kite conceded, she walked it to a flag hitching post where children had tied their kites earlier in the day. The next morning, Madison flew the kite at dawn then again at dusk, walking it like a dog on a leash. This became her new ritual for that first week in Gulf Shores. She wrestled her guilt with the heavens through the kite strings Rhett had so firmly built.

Bygones

Madison often compartmentalized very uncomfortable things, putting them into neat little bundles and labeling them bygones. It was easier to form the unspoken words from mouths of cowards or write the proper ending to the unfinished. That was where Madison was mistaken. She assumed the outcome with Lane could have been different.

129

Madison got the guest room ready for Lane's visit. She drove into town to buy groceries and lots of alcohol. She was twisting Lane's guilt with her civility. Madison knew there were deep issues welling to the surface that had to be addressed. They swirled around her head, a halo of verbal garbage and debris. She feared her interaction would be violent and unladylike. Madison had always been a master at controlling her emotions. She now purged them as they washed over her in waves; anger bubbled like a witch's brew, betrayal bled, red and hot, while guilt clung like fog around corners.

Madison was chilling a bottle of chardonnay as the engine on Lane's silver Z3 convertible could be heard pulling into the drive. Lane knocked on the wooden screen door frame, the only thing separating the two. She gripped her duffle bag stringently. Madison ushered Lane down the hallway, pushing the door to the guest room open very glibly. Lane tossed her duffle bag in the dusty corner. Her footsteps were laborious as she approached Madison on the deck. Madison nodded to a half empty bottle of wine, nursing her own glass. Lane poured a large glass, admiring the view of the ocean. The two just shared the same space, letting the liquor warm their toes. Seagulls danced over small children for their breadcrumbs. Storm clouds brewed on the peaceful skyline horizon.

"I didn't come all this way for silence, Madison. Who slaps first?"

Madison was firm, rigid. Her personal space surrounded with barbed wire.

"Don't temp me."

Madison had her anger caged around her tightly.

"Let's start with my sins...Big, bad, evil Lane."

Lane's temper raged in her voice, a spring wound too tightly, abruptly popping out in her inflection and mannerisms.

"Fine -why *did* you sleep with Rhett?"

"You know what I'll say...it's complicated. You lived it, too."

Lane turned away, clenching her fists in aggravation.

Madison spun Lane around. They were face to face. Madison's eyes shot a glower very sadly into Lane's soul.

"We can do this all night, Lane. We can banter back and forth or we can just beat the shit out of each other."

Madison pushed Lane's shoulder with her quick fingertips.

"I don't want to fight you, Madison."

"I didn't give you a choice, now did I?"

Madison thrust her wine onto Lane's face, slamming the glass onto the deck where it splintered into dangerous pebbles. Lane opened her mouth to speak, but the only sound audible was her throat sucking air. She had been ambushed.

"Why are you working with Vincent after everything I did for you?"

"He *blackmailed* me. Before I knew you, Madison, Vincent blackmailed me into sleeping with Rhett!"

"Since when has a little blackmail ever stopped you?!"

"Vincent had *things* on me that would get me disowned from my family…you know how that works."

Madison pushed Lane backwards more forcefully. Lane defended, lunging and wrapping her hands around Madison's throat. She slammed Madison against the screen door. Lane's black mafia eyes bore down on Madison firmly. Heavy wine breaths churned like a locomotive from both women's anxiety. Lane loosened her grip. As Madison stopped fighting, the mania retreated from Lane's stare. Lane's frenzy morphed into passion. Her small hands that had throttled Madison just seconds before cupped Madison's cheeks and she softly kissed Madison on the lips. This was a different kind of obsession that converted the kiss, making it grow ravenous and wet. Lane abruptly pulled away. Her lipstick was smeared around the perimeter of Madison's full mouth, their eyes locked in limbo.

"I wanted to wreck your marriage.
Can't you see?

I've always wanted *you*."

Lane ran her fingertips down
Madison's hips.

"I still want you."

Madison skeptically studied Lane's
body language. She brushed Lane's sticky,
wine-soaked hair behind her ear, grabbing
her throat.

"Don't get too comfortable with *my*
things."

Moonlight Madness

Madison walked down to the end of
the boardwalk, sitting on the steps. Dusk
was always more alluring on the beach,
especially on nights with a full moon. She
watched the moon's reflection wiggle on the
water. It amazed her how certain people
crafted and stirred different facets. Madison
had Lane pegged in ways Lane could hide
from others rather easily. Lane had learned
Madison's ways, understanding her

motivations and fears. They were equally matched and that terrified Madison.

A silhouette walked across the moonlit path, startling Madison's fixation. She flinched.

"I'm sorry. I didn't mean to scare you."

"It is so late. I thought I was alone."

Madison knew the voice, saw his cropped hair now dark spikes in the moonlight. Houston's skin smelled of soap, freshly bathed.

"Are you OK?"

"I just buried my husband."

Madison was stoic, gawking at the moon.

Houston put his hands in his jean short pockets, processing her earlier kite display in a different light.

"A grieving woman shouldn't be out alone this time of night."

"I'm not that kind of woman."

Madison crossed her arms, hypnotized by the moon. Houston turned around, poised to walk back down the beach

135

toward his house and leave her in the moon's grip.

"If you ever need... to throw up on someone's boardwalk again..."

He motioned in the direction of his home. Madison grimaced, putting her face in her hands.

"Ugh.... Thanks."

As she walked back up the boardwalk to the beach house, Madison caught a glimpse of Lane's shadow through the glass door. She was rifling through the red folder that contained Rhett's will. Lane cradled her cell phone under her neck as she put the will back in Madison's briefcase, disappearing down the hallway to her room. Madison floated fastidiously toward the guest room, catching Lane's muffled ending sentences.

"I haven't spoken to her about the will. I don't think she has located it yet. You have to give me time. I just got here and didn't receive a warm reception thanks to you...no, no... I've got to go."

Madison lobbed open Lane's bedroom door. Lane was lying on her stomach in a t-shirt and panties, sprawled across the bed as she snapped her cell phone shut, ending her conversation. Madison leaned into the door frame, crossing her arms. Lane tossed the phone onto the floor in exasperation.

"He *just* won't leave me alone."

A beaded line of perspiration formed on Lane's upper lip. Madison could see the veins in Lane's neck throbbing.

"Goodnight."

Madison turned off the light and shut the door.

Where There is a Will

Things that stew tend to build to a force that is seismic. Lane was lying, and Madison's own anger and rage was becoming difficult to harness. It had taken all their strength not to come to blows.

Madison dreamed of Houston. They were walking along the beach, the water coming in and out over their bare feet. Shells and debris lined their path and they had to dodge their sharpness. Madison was telling Houston very personal, private things about her strange life as he held her arm, protecting and balancing her along the swift tides. He just listened. His eyes were soft with compassion, his smile reassuring. As they approached her boardwalk, Houston told Madison she had to face her fears. In that instant, Houston morphed into Lane. She was holding Madison's hands and leaning in to kiss her. Madison awoke, sweating, clutching her blanket tightly, her hair wringing wet. She ran out onto her bedroom balcony. Her body was clammy underneath her cotton nightshirt. Smoke trails danced under Madison's nose. She looked down to see Lane standing on the deck below, smoking a cigarette. Madison addressed the smoke trail.

"I thought you quit?"

"I did."

Lane smelled Madison's perfume in the humid midnight hour.

Madison walked back to her bed, curling up under the thin cotton sheets. She dozed in and out of sleep, her mind racing. Like mist, Lane appeared. She sat on the floor, sipping a glass of chardonnay, just helplessly watching Madison. The light of the moon lent a purple hue to Madison's fair face.

Then, she stood over Madison, consuming the proximity, marveling in the syncopation in her breathing. Lane brushed Madison's hair away from her face, stroking her cheek with the back of her hand. She leaned in and kissed Madison evenly on the lips. Madison pressed her lips together, tasting the wine Lane was drinking.

"I think I'm in love with you. I've always been."

Lane's words bounced around her mouth like marbles.

Lane heard Madison sigh heavily in the darkness. She ran her hands down Madison's shoulder and arm, just wanting to touch her, be near her and coax forgiveness out of her pores. Madison reached for

Lane's fingers, halting her caress. Lane began to cry. Madison opened her arms to Lane, and she curled up, weeping in Madison's security. Madison held Lane as she cried, letting her feed on her softness, weakening her in order to find out her secrets. Lane cried herself to sleep in Madison's arms. Madison suppressed her own anger, her own tears.

Lane slept next to Madison. Madison watched the clock with every hour. She spied the sun's fury rising through the late August haze. Her phone beeped with a text message. *I miss you, Momma. I love you. Hannah.*

Madison walked to the deck with her phone, taking a picture of the waves, sending it to Hannah. *Soon Hannah… I love you. Momma*

Madison brewed dark, strong coffee. Flashes of their convoluted night made Madison shudder. Lane's hands had strayed in her conflict, roving Madison's skin with unnerving breaches of boundaries as she practically forced herself on Madison. Madison had patiently deflected Lane's drunken advances, ushering her roaming fingers back into fists. Lane knew how to suspend valued information in order to selfishly get what she wanted. Her own manipulation by her family had created the exploitive behavior.

The morning light haloed Lane's eyes that bore deep black rings from her drunkenness. She stumbled to the coffee Madison had made. Madison stared into her cup, cautiously watching Lane's body language. Lane moved with calculated agility.

"Tell me what is so important in Rhett's will that Vincent must know?"

Lane watched Madison sip her coffee, her knuckles white with the grip on the handle. Lane turned evasive.

"What are you insinuating?"

Lane looked at the table in anger. Her tightly wound clock springs began to creak and pop. Lane stared into Madison's eyes, finding only cool, steely blue staring back.

"I saw you rifling through my briefcase last night. Why did you *not* tell Vincent I had the will?"

"I don't know what you are talking about...I love you."

Madison was trembling again, molten lava bubbling under the surface.

"Oh, don't go making this about love - you narcissistic bitch. This doesn't have anything to do with it. It is all about your money. You're not in this for me. You are always in over your head for *you*."

Lane threw open the patio door, rattling its hinges with conceit, bellowing out onto the deck. Madison charged hot on her heels.

Madison grabbed the back of Lane's shirt, manipulating her skinny frame. Lane defended wildly, punching Madison with a frenzied force that only incited more fury. Madison heaved Lane over the rail and into the sand, rushing her on the offensive.

"You took Hannah and you gave her away without my knowledge. Did you do that out of love?!"

Lane jumped up as blood poured from her head. She steam-rolled Madison and pinned her wrists to the sand, straddling her. Lane's head began to rapidly drop daubs of blood onto Madison's face. Both women were breathing like prizefighters.

"Rhett cut Vincent out of everything they had worked on together. Rhett has bounced the shit all around. Vincent can't find it. He is coming after you for what you know, and he's using Hannah. I'm trying to protect you both!"

Lane released Madison's wrists only to get punched in the stomach. As Lane fell backward in agony, Madison scrambled in the sand, turning her back to Lane as she clung to the side of the boardwalk. Lane saddled Madison. Madison lunged wildly, trying to throw her off, but Lane had a death grip, fastening her arms under Madison's armpits like the straps of a back pack. She wrapped her legs firmly around Madison's

143

waist. Madison bucked like a wild bronco as Lane squeezed her guts intermittently with her knees.

It was mid-morning and beachgoers were just starting to appear. Houston was on his walk. From a distance, the two women looked like children playing, but as Houston got closer he noticed the fight ensuing. He ran closer, seeing that it was Madison trying desperately to free another woman from her back. Houston interjected, grabbing Lane, who was scratching and clawing at him in retaliation. Houston freed Madison, holding Lane at bay. Madison regained her composure only to take the opportunity to fist a handful of sand and throw it in Lane's face.

"That is for kissing me!"

Houston restrained Lane as she spit out clumps of sand. He followed Madison, walking Lane to the deck. Madison noticed blood on Houston's arm where Lane had cut him.

"You're bleeding. I'm sorry."

"What about me?"

Lane gawked at her scratches as blood oozed from her forehead.

"What about you?"

Houston grinned, understanding Madison's unpredictable behavior more clearly. Madison was a fine-tuned machine. She channeled the steam at the right time mastering endurance. Lane ran on adrenaline, sporadic and random. Houston smiled at both ladies. He walked away, watching the tension ricochet from woman to woman.

After Blows

There was stifling stillness in the minutes after the brawl. Madison had walked into the beach house and fallen onto the couch, exhausted before the day had truly begun. Lane perched on the steps leading to the boardwalk. Her bleeding head in her hands as she replayed the words hurled like daggers between two women that had both been hurt deeply. There was agony that projected further than their treachery. It

145

spewed out of their eyes and actions, a powder keg of pent-up hostility that had showered the beach like rain.

Madison noticed the blood and dirt on her hands and arms. She ran warm water on a rag and examined her painted war face in the bathroom mirror. Lane's blood was mingled with her own in spatters across her nose, creating bloody freckles. The patio door creaked horrendously as Lane finally entered. Neither spoke, sharing the explosive air. They examined the other's sorrow in their mismatched cuts and bruises.

Lane sat with her head in her hands as Madison moved nearer the proximity charged with positive and negative energies as Madison finished wiping blood from her arms and face. Lane's arms resembled a leper, scarred and hideous. Madison put her hand on Lane's shoulder, stroking Lane's coarse dark brown hair. She wiped blood and dirt from Lane's wounds. Lane's forehead had dark, dried blood on the cut Madison had inflicted. She dabbed it with a mother's care as Lane closed her eyes.

Madison's intuition was fine-tuned; she could smell fear and secrets in another's warm breath.

"This hurts you, doesn't it – to be this close to me and let me clean your wounds?"

Madison watched Lane's tears build. Lane touched Madison's hand, halting her kindness.

"This is why you didn't tell me about Hannah. You wanted me to hurt like you are hurting."

"I love you, Madison. This isn't part of an act. I never meant for *things* to happen this way."

"I know."

Madison pulled Lane into her embrace. Madison's safety loosened Lane's tongue.

"Vincent is up to something big, dangerous. I need more time. I only know that Hannah is our shared vulnerability."

Neighbor children screamed with joy, splashing loudly in the pool next door. Lane noticed the tension in their exchanges.

Betrayal laced every intimacy. It was always in the background, tainting their progress.

"You know, Lane, in order to make *things* go away, we have to get rid of the threat."

"It's not that simple with Vincent."

"It can be…if you want it."

There was the promise of finality in Madison's words. Lane realized the reason Madison tolerated her. They needed each other. Their partnering held a new beginning.

Section III

Where There Is Smoke
September 2007

Smoke signals can be invisible. But, people who have survived similar blazes can see them and recognize the signals. Since Madison took up residency, she had been fanning signals from her own never-ending fire. Houston was allured by the embers.

Madison was reading the newspaper, enjoying a very black cup of coffee after a long, hard night of active dreams. The dreams were like watching a movie of her life. She was an observer, appalled and disturbed at the utter slaughter of the innocent and unaware, betrayed by their own. The realities she had coped with and lived through in her marriage were working themselves out. Lane and Madison had buried the hatchet in shallow sand. Their sincerity was still very surface and uncharted. She hoped September promised something better.

Her thoughts disintegrated as she startled with the ringing of the house phone.

"Madison, it's your neighbor Houston. I was just checking in on you."

Madison exhaled with embarrassment as she remembered the catfight he had interceded only a week earlier.

"I meant to call and apologize after that scene. I'd rather just forget about it."

Houston remembered her walking the beach that first evening. Madison had secrets just in the way she sauntered.

"I'm going to take a walk on the beach…"

"…and you'd like to see if I can do something other than vomit or fight?"

"If you feel I'm imposing I'll leave you alone. It's just…I lost someone close a long time ago…Sometimes it is…too quiet."

There was silence on the line, hesitation and fear fresh from tragedy and Madison's former way of living.

"I usually fly my kite at seven just before sunset. Feel free to join me."

Houston began walking west toward Madison's house. The sunset was more yellow this young September evening, hinting autumn. The silent change of season showed in the sun's trajectory that was almost perfectly parallel with the shoreline.

Houston reached the kite post but Madison wasn't there. He smelled her lotion in the humid evening air. He looked to her house and she waved from the porch steps. As he approached, Madison pointed to the table on the patio where a bucket chilled a bottle of chardonnay.

Madison wore little makeup and her hair was pulled away from her face. He admired the fine lines of experience that traced her crystal eyes. They walked adjacent, maneuvering between the tide and the thicker sand. There was a shared intimacy in their silence, an unspoken energy they balanced when closing the day together. As they turned around, the wind blew through Houston's clothes, giving Madison that clean hint of soap. Back at Madison's boardwalk, they awkwardly glanced and averted their gaze. Both found words untrustworthy.

They walked the long boardwalk to
Madison's porch where the chardonnay
chilled. Both fleetingly studied the sand
dune where Houston had torn Lane from
Madison. Madison reached for the
chardonnay, pouring them each a glass. She
gravitated to the long, wide step of the patio.
Houston threw out small oyster crackers that
he always carried in his pocket for the
seagulls.

"How did your husband die?"

Houston watched the seagulls dance
over him, anticipating more crackers.

"He was murdered."

Madison gulped her wine. Her
anxiety emptied the glass quickly.

"I saw you fly that kite the first night
you arrived."

He offered her more wine. She put
down her glass, lacing her fingers tightly,
making a fist. She squeezed her hands
together in a pacifying rhythm.

"Am I making you uncomfortable?"

She ran her trembling fingers
through her hair in aggravation.

154

"No. I'm just all kinds of hell right now. I just keep waiting to wake up and this all be a dream."

He poured her more wine. Houston saw much more than sorrow through the many layered walls to her soul.

"Some days are harder, Madison."

Madison beat on her chest until her sobs were a whisper.

"It's been a hard life."

Houston sat beside her on the wide step. The erratic southerly breeze tangled the scents of their skin, making their tragedies now akin.

"That weight lessens over time…that life fades."

The walk and the wine would become their September ritual. The two listened to the tides whisper long after the wine was gone. Madison embraced the solace in his well-timed silences.

Houston King

Madison's husband died, yet I feel much more surrounding her than grief. I watched her emotional baggage fall to the sand with the slam of the car door the first night she appeared. There is a story in Madison's posture. She wears her pride like a mink stole. She doesn't just walk. She persuades.

She would have killed this friend and enemy that appeared like a grey shadow if she hadn't learned how to balance her grace and concern. Madison's nuance was full of bitterness and compassion diplomatically equalized. This person is one of many tragic pieces to Madison's mysterious puzzle.

I am drawn to Madison even though I have been burned by similar blazes. I've lost, walked her journey in my past and selfishly, horribly mangled it. I don't believe in chance. A man makes his choices. This feels different. She is different. Her kite flight is fraught with contradictions. Our like paths crossed and appear to be timed appropriately. I want to know her.

Madison is mesmerized with the vastness and enormity of the sea. She is of the salt and dirt of her world. She smells vulnerable and reeks of danger. I've always found the scent of a woman rather telling.

Some of the Old

Old *things* resurface to remind us
who we are and who we once were. No
amount of water from the never ending tides
can wash away the stains or the regrets of
the past. Stitches only keep a wound closed
so time can heal the wound. The scar is the
constant reminder.

Madison checked her email for the
first time since arriving. In her former life,
it was a morning ritual. It was mid-
afternoon and she scrolled through an insane
triple digit number of messages in her inbox.
Most were condolences from Rhett's former
clientele. One stood out in particular. It was
from Dyer. The email was a week old, and
email was hardly his style. The subject line
read *Hannah's First Day*. She tapped her
fingernails on the desk before clicking on
the email.

The photo was of Hannah's first day
of school. Her hair was pulled half back and
she was dressed in black leggings and a pink
top. She carried a purple backpack on her

right shoulder. Hannah's smile was widely pronounced, ensuring the recipient noticed her missing two front teeth. She had changed so much in a month. Dyer had written Madison a short note:

Madison ~ you asked me to keep you posted on our girl. She got $5 from the tooth fairy for those front teeth. She misses you. I miss you. I hate crowds. They are so lonely. ~Dyer

She reached for her cell phone.

"I got the picture today. I haven't been checking my mail. How was Hannah's first day?"

"She loves school…It's good to hear your voice."

Silence ensued for an uncomfortable interval.

"I'm sorry I didn't call sooner…Dyer, I didn't know how much *this* hurt. You're a good man."

"Don't get ahead of yourself."

Madison sounded lost in her sorrow, searching for a life vest to float her dark waters. Dyer recognized the weariness in her half-hearted chuckle.

"You love Hannah for me."

"I try. No one can love her quite like you."

She could almost touch Hannah's rosy, soft cheeks. Madison rewound Vincent's comment about little girls' necks snapping. Her precious Hannah Beth caught in the middle of the monster of a life she had dragged Dyer through. Guilt ransacked her conscience.

"I'm just so sorry...for everything."

"Don't be. I'm not."

It was almost kite flying hour and she had asked Houston to accompany her. She stared at the computer and began searching *Houston King*. Up came *Woodruff and King Oil*. The first website had a picture of Houston many years earlier followed by his biography. Houston had built his oil company from the ground. He had lived in Dallas, had been married with a daughter. Houston's smile flashed confidence despite his crooked and boyish teeth now white and straight.

Madison searched Houston's ex-wife, *Caroline King*. Headlines abounded. Little toy soldiers of truth lined up scandal in the Dallas papers. She had been convicted of murdering a former partner of *Woodruff and King*. Seems Caroline had a personality disorder. The details were sketchy. Madison shut down her laptop.

Half a mile down the beach, Houston closed his search engine on a very dark, telling page. Madison was still very emotionally tethered to her not yet former life. She wasn't implicated in any of her dead husband's brushes with dishonor. Rhett Peacock had a case history that lacked morality, a sleaze of a lawyer.

The Strings Attached

Madison sat on the steps at the end of her boardwalk, waiting for Houston. She fidgeted with the strings to Rhett's kite, untangling them from the mess the wind had made of them the day before.

"Looks like the kite took you for a ride."

Houston stared at Madison as she concentrated on the mangled ball of string. She handed it to him.

"I give up. I think I need the wine first."

Houston methodically unraveled the knot and the strings came apart easily. He handed the kite to Madison. She put her hands on her hips, jealous of his efficiency.

"Well, looks like you've done this before."

"Made the mess or straightened it?"

Houston saw what appeared to be a genuine grin form out of her distraction.

She trotted a bit to get the kite into the air, giving it more string as it danced to lofty heights. He watched Madison maneuver it to the left and the right making its beautiful, hypnotic tail dance.

"You really show that kite who is boss."

163

"There are so many strings attached. You have to know just the right way to pull it or it will crash and take you with it."

Her long, slender fingers and hands were deceptively fragile, their strength revealed when she reeled the kite to her, taming it before she let it soar.

"Are you just learning this or have you always known how to pull strings?"

"Rhett taught me all I know. I never got to play with his toys until now."

"How's that working for you?"

"You tell me."

"You look like you can handle your own."

"Looks are always deceiving."

Madison's eyes were wild, fierce.

Houston reached in his pocket, throwing out oyster crackers for the seagulls. They made their way back to Madison's patio and the wine. He stared oddly at the letter.

"I think we had a visitor."

Houston pointed to the note. She fumbled the wine bottle to Houston,

164

snatching the letter with vehemence. Her name was typed with an old typewriter she knew well. The M struck higher than the rest of the letters. She tore it open to find a picture of Hannah playing in her own backyard and at school with her friends. The next photo was Dyer kissing a young woman. The final photo was what appeared to be freshly dug graves. There was a type-written note: *Just catchin' you up on our little gurl…This is what happens to those who betray.* Madison's neck flushed. She carefully placed the photos back into the envelope. Houston watched her labored control.

"Some of the strings attached to that kite of your husband's?"

Madison boldly handed him the envelope. Houston thumbed through the pictures.

"The child is the string you're fighting."

"Why are you here? What do you want?"

"I don't want anything. It's just that I've been here...done this."

"Done *this*?"

"Dragged a woman through hell over a child she couldn't have."

Madison ripped the pictures from his fingers and sprinted away. Houston watched Madison fight his fated facts. Her quick steps pounded the boardwalk. Muffled sobs rumbled as she buried her face in her knees. Houston sauntered to Madison, standing with his hands in his pockets, turning the oyster crackers over and over. She had thrown the depraved pictures in the sand. Houston picked them up and blew the sand from the smiling child's photo.

"What's her name?"

"Hannah."

"I have a daughter...her mother was very protective of her...kind of like you."

"What's your point?"

"Her real mother wasn't my wife."

Madison lunged at his knees, knocking him into the sand. He had finally incited all things dark and wrathful that she so eloquently ruled. He groaned, astounded at her strength.

"You're a dangerous woman."

"You have no idea just how much."

Madison offered her hand to him and they once again headed back to the wine. He shook the sand from his back and Madison wiped snotty tears that had chased her weaknesses down her chin. She cradled the picture of Hannah. Houston took the more disturbing photos that Madison was holding and put them under the ice bucket.

"Let's just put these on ice for now."

Houston uncorked the wine, taking a long drink from the bottle before handing it to Madison. She stared suspiciously at where his lips had been.

"I've got this dance class tomorrow night...want to join me...no strings attached to these feet."

"What? I don't even *like* you!"

"Most people don't."

Madison turned up the wine bottle. Houston began walking away.

"I'll pick you up at seven."

She growled, kicking sand in his direction.

"Don't use *me* to right your wrongs!"

Houston's lengthy strides curtly ceased. He mouthed over his shoulder.

"You're nothing like my wrongs."

Old Ghosts

Madison put the photos away, finally crawling into bed after finishing off the wine. The humidity soothed her this evening. She left her bedroom windows cracked slightly.

The smell of cigar roused her from sleep. She looked toward the windows and saw a silhouette seated in her easy chair. It's tall, fat head was smoking.

"You shouldn't leave your windows open. Someone can come crawlin' right in."

Madison had nothing to say to him.

"I've been talkin' to Lane. She said the will is going to be finalized come Thanksgivin'. You were real generous

168

floatin' me some cash since my family bailed on me."

"Cut to it, Vincent."

"See, I know you are searchin' for the account with the money that Rhett and I stole together. I just want you to know that I expect you to find that information by the readin' of the will."

"I'm doing my best."

"Are you? A smart business man uses and *abuses* the best resources available."

Vincent puffed a large smoke ring, laughing.

"People are going to start sufferin'."

"Get out."

Sway

The utter thought of dancing again frightened Madison, sending nervous chills up her neck and arms. Dancing didn't come naturally for her. When Houston shot his eyes to the extremes, Madison noticed familiar glints of regret not apparent in his

169

straightforward gaze. He was a master at keeping his pain in the far corners. His candor rivaled Madison's many masks.

Houston's 1969 black on black Corvette hardtop convertible could be heard purring as he pulled into the sandy drive. The sun was low on the horizon, bouncing golden sunshine off his freshly waxed car. He was wearing black sunglasses and his light hair stood out like a rebel. Houston opened her door. Madison met him with a fussy grimace.

Madison put her sunglasses on, smiling at Houston as he fastened his seat belt. He punched the gas and the rear end fishtailed, throwing sand two feet in the air. The thinning humidity of mid-September combed their hair with promises of cooler days. They listened to the hum of the road as slow jazz played on the radio. He was wearing cologne. She was wearing perfume.

The dance academy was small and personal with old-fashioned hardwood floors. Other dancers were chatting when the two of them walked into the room. They had arrived last and the teacher clapped her arthritic, bony hands together. Silence ensued. The teacher instructed them to assume their positions then put the needle on the record of her very old turntable.

Madison and Houston touched intimately for the first time as they assumed their pose, listening to the pop and crackle of the needle. Feelings flowed through their now braided fingers as their eyes connected. Madison's arms were rigid, her heart a jet engine. Her susceptibility glared in the down turn of her lips, tight and fearful. Houston smiled at her.

The music started. The first step was on the downbeat as they fell into the dance with a plunge and a splash just like the first time they had met. Madison and Houston hit the pendulum motions of the dance rather symmetrically with their feet working in sync. Houston spun Madison with force, testing her wrists with his precision. Madison fought to secure truths with her tight full lips that were parted slightly. Houston jutted left then right,

171

taunting her like the kite. Madison pulled him right then left, challenging his agility. The old dance teacher admired their combustibility.

The final dance for the evening was the rumba; it was a romantic, sexy dance. When the music began, Madison's lips slanted a crooked grin in one corner. Fear changed to danger. She moved her hips as if she were writing her name with them in large flowing cursive. Her eyes were lost in some bedroom past. Houston bit his lower lip. His pupils dilated as his eyes narrowed like a fox watching his prey. Houston's prowess showed by the very small, quick and precise swishes he made with his pelvis. When the dance ended, the pair was sweating and breathing heavily. The old spinster smiled; her aged teeth endeared her wrinkled dimples. In a motherly fashion, she patted Houston on the back, cutting her eyes in acceptance of his new partner. Houston handed Madison his handkerchief and she wiped sweat from her brow.

Houston's hand rested on the small of her back.

What Now?

The sun had set, leaving a blue-gray cast over the landscape as Houston drove Madison back to her beach house. Madison had emoted on the dance floor but now pulled away. There was a chain link fence surrounding her. He could only reach so far into her. The hum of the corvette's tires filled their silence.

They arrived and Houston put the car in park. They listened to the engine purr for an eternal instant. Madison stared out someplace much farther than the beach. Houston fished her eyes for signals. Madison looked at him with an ache he understood. She opened the car door as Houston shut down the engine. He wondered where her eyes were taking him.

Madison retrieved two *Rolling Rock* beers from the refrigerator and led Houston to the patio. He leaned over the railing, entranced by the sound of the waves. Waves that called him, called Madison inward.

"Thanks for tonight. It was a nice distraction."

"Was it?"

Tears shimmered on Madison's cheekbones.

"I've still got a lot of work to do."

Houston reached for her cheek and wiped her mascara tears with his thumb. He had never touched Madison. Her skin was supple, her cheeks warm with adrenaline.

"You're a tough girl."

Impending Storms

Madison spread a blanket on the sand. They lay silently staring up at the stars. She fell asleep beside him, secure in his confidence. Houston cased the perimeters of the night for that shifty stranger that had been lurking around her new home.

Balmy winds blew the back of
Houston's shirt open, tickling his spine.
Madison pursed her lips unconsciously,
keeping the blowing sand out of her mouth.
He shook her slightly, trying to rouse her
from sleep.

Houston got little response as the
wind accelerated its brief bursts into a
constant, more powerful gust. He stood,
wrapping Madison in his arms, letting the
blanket fly down the beach. Madison didn't
stir. Her head bobbed up and down as her
body fought his beach rescue. When he
finally got into the house, he examined
Madison in his arms. Her hair and face were
dotted with sand, her mouth agape.

Houston laid Madison onto her bed.
He went into the bathroom and found a cloth
and soap. He returned and wiped the sand
from her cheeks and lips. Its force had
almost driven it into her pores. He brushed
her hair away from her face. Her brow
began wrinkling a perfectly defined line;
distress carved such definition. She ran her

fingers through her hair, looking around the room and finally at Houston.

"What happened?"

"A storm."

"How did I get here?"

"I carried you."

Madison felt gritty from the sandstorm. She pulled at her clothes. They were disheveled and ill-fitted from Houston hurriedly scooping her up. The top of her right breast was visible through her bulging top. He reached over and pulled her shirt closed, respecting her organized panic. She examined her surroundings. He studied her face, her gestures.

"Who's following you?"

Thunder rumbled in the distance, followed by lightning that illuminated the beach. Houston noticed a tall figure standing by the kite post, smoking.

Section IV

The Storm
October 2007

Houston didn't sleep, opening the patio door and letting the warm breeze blow through the screen as the storm echoed gentle thunder and rain. It danced off the rooftop as the thin windows rattled harshly. Madison slept fitfully, tossing and turning and talking at times the strange language of a child.

Houston rubbed his eyes. He sipped coffee and peered out the bedroom window as the sunrise fought to break the murkiness, analyzing Madison's posture as she slept. Her nose and lips twitched. The house phone rang. Houston hustled into the kitchen to answer it. His hello was greeted by heavy, restless breathing. He quietly hung up.

Madison roused and was gazing at the ceiling, her features soft and her eyes puffy. Houston eased back to her room and stood in the doorway.

"Good morning, tough girl."

Houston offered her his coffee. She took the cup, sipping it curiously, looking at him over the rim. She let a smile slip.

Madison's cell phone rang and her slight smile fell to the floor. Men had sharpened her edges, making her curt. She cut a shooing glance to Houston and he left. She cleared her throat to answer. He walked to the patio, noticing her intonation and voice were cold and firm. Men had in turn ground her prowess to a fine point, heightening her aptness.

Madison snapped the phone shut, joining Houston. She was now a different woman than a moment ago. He watched her swallow hard, pushing distress back down into her guts. He could no longer see her gentle seams.

"You really love that little girl, don't you? You'd do anything to protect her."

Madison didn't respond. Her left eye twitched. Houston connected the gravity of her visitor with her deeply furrowed brow.

"A long time ago I did *anything* in order to protect my daughter. It cost me everything…except her."

"I'm all she's got."

"She's all that *you've* got. That is why you'll do whatever it takes."

Houston watched Madison pace. Her mind was explosively turning over his words, forging trust that ricocheted between their denim blue eyes. Houston bit his lower lip, finding the sludge that was dragging him into her spellbinding.

Brown Boxes and Broken Kites

There was a knock on Madison's screen door. She found a parcel package on her step. It was basic brown with no return address. Madison closed her eyes, setting the small box on the kitchen counter. Her mind raced mafia-style, deducing the package was too small to house any body parts other than fingers, toes, or eyeballs. She tore open the box lid.

Inside was a crumpled Arkansas newspaper dated a few days back. She emptied the box onto the counter. Out fell a pink barrette with a pigtail of blond hair clipped into it. She put the pigtail to her nose, gently placing it on the counter, straightening it as if it were still attached to Hannah's head. Wrapped in another clump of paper was an empty wallet, well worn with merely a photo of Madison in a far pocket. She recognized it. It was Dyer's wallet. Madison had helped Hannah pick it out for his birthday. The tidal waves began to roar a deafening howl of danger, crashing onto Madison's shore.

Houston was meeting Madison for the walk and wine. She flew the kite alone today thinking about Vincent's lurking aggressiveness. His plans hinted fruition with his threatening immediacy. Madison had been averting the account number for two weeks.

She fought the wind as September bled into October rather violently with storms and winds even a kite master wouldn't dare. Madison had decided to reel in the kite when it hit. A gust so strong it pulled the controls out of her grasp. The kite danced in frenzied circles before beginning a spiraled descent. It crashed with fury into the sand, landing 100 yards downwind from Madison. She rushed to it and it was broken in many places. She gathered up the pieces and rushed to her patio, string tangled over her back and shoulders, cradling Rhett's broken prize. She laid it on the patio table, pushing the wine bucket aside. Pieces had cracked and broken everywhere. She picked up the strongest limb of the kite now warped and fragile. It snapped in her fingers, falling into a million bits. With a whimper, she pronounced the kite dead.

Houston found her crying at her patio table, the kite in ruins.

"I tried to save it."

Madison picked up a limp, broken arm. When she did, a small silver bullet Rhett had used to hide information fell out of the broken end and rolled on the smooth decking, stopping at Houston's feet. He picked it up and tossed it to her.

She opened the end and pulled out a rolled up piece of paper. Typed on it was a series of numbers. One was an account number and the other a phone number and address.

"I'm not ready!! Do you hear me??!"

Madison's lips were intense, her hands trembling as she punched at Rhett in the heavens.

"What just happened?"

She motioned Houston inside the house where she showed him the package that arrived earlier.

"Whose are these?"

"Hannah and her father... He and Hannah were my... patients."

Madison's remorseful eyes painted a bond. She ran her finger tips across the smooth, well worn leather wallet affectionately.

"He's going to kill them...for *this*. I have to protect them."

184

Houston placed the wine glass into her hand as he kissed her fingers, simultaneously coaxing the silver bullet from her. He slid it into his pocket, mixing it with the oyster crackers.

Imminent Danger

Houston left to get more wine. Madison stood on the patio, watching him until he disappeared from view. A strange chill ran through Madison's body and the hair on the back of her neck stood on end. She rubbed the chill from her shoulders when a hand covered her mouth and forcibly restrained her. He was tall and burly, hiding his face with a ski mask. His fingers were cupped professionally as she tried to bite them as he overpowered her, dragging her into the house.

He pushed her onto the kitchen floor, pulling rope from his pocket, his breaths labored with frustration. Madison charged the door and he tripped her with his large boot, grabbing her shirt and ripping it half off as he slapped her savagely, cutting her cheekbone. Madison flailed her arms unsuccessfully and he kneed her in the stomach, forcing her surrender.

Madison's nose bled steadily as the intruder tied her to a chair, cutting her wrists and ankles with his heated knots. Then, Vincent removed the mask and examined his handy work on her cherry cheek. She sniffed hard, trying to stop the blood from running down her lips and chin.

"I am serious about hurtin' people."

Vincent fidgeted with his phone as her blood rushed like raindrops onto the floor. He dialed his voicemail, putting it on speakerphone. Lane's voice began.

"Vincent, I got the money transferred for you....But, I haven't found Rhett's will...I don't know if Madison has found it yet...But, I've at least kept my end of the bargain. You have to keep yours... Please."

Vincent snapped the phone shut.

"Lane is lyin'."

Madison stared at the floor.

"You have what I want. I've waited ten years for this."

Vincent knelt to her level. Madison spit blood in his face. He yanked the back of her hair and smacked her cheek harder, pulling her gaze toward his. They were inches apart, eye to eye. He thrust her head forward like a rag doll.

"You've got til Thanksgivin'."

Houston marched up Madison's boardwalk when he saw their stranger closing the patio door and pulling his ball cap low on his tall, fat profile. He poised the wine bottle like a weapon, running in pursuit, but the shadow had cleverly disintegrated.

Houston threw Madison's door open, rattling the window frames. He found Madison tied to a chair, her head bobbling. She wept as he untied her arms and legs. Deep, raw rope burns indicated the force used while securing the knots. He eased her into his arms and carried her to the couch, wiping blood from her face with his bare hands. Her cheek was bruised and beginning to swell. Dilemma grew precious and urgent as he cradled her badly battered face.

Madison heard his distinct voice grumble as he stepped into the other room. She prayed they were still alone. Her mouth formed a well managed straight line as she feigned composure. She was slipping in and out of consciousness and didn't hear him return to her side. His weighty stare revived her.

"I called a doctor friend of mine."

"I don't need your charity."

"I don't consider Mafia *charity*."

Madison swung at Houston. He had anticipated her punch, catching her hand as it careened toward his groin. He stared compassionately into her shameful eyes.

The doctor arrived within the hour to check Madison's injuries. Houston knew she would need a few stitches to the cut on her cheekbone. He left the female doctor alone with Madison. She introduced herself merely as 'Cassandra', eyeballing

Madison's cheek with a frown. She dug
through her bag for the suture kit.

"Think that needs a stitch, dear."
Madison flinched at the doctor's fast-
fingered needlework.
"How do you know Houston?"

"He volunteers and supports a lot of
programs where I am involved."
The doctor spoke cautiously, respecting
Houston's privacy.

She lifted Madison's shirt, revealing
huge bruises. She probed Madison's ribs.
Madison appeared fairly comfortable with
her touch.

"I don't think anything is fractured.
Call me if something changes and I will
meet you at my office."

She smiled and handed Madison her
card. Madison stared at the floor in
humiliation.

"Confidentially, I don't do house
calls for just anyone."

Cassandra patted Madison's knee,
passing over the unspoken with nuggets of
sincerity.

189

Houston stood in the doorway with his hands in his pockets. The imaginary line in the sand was now drawn. Madison patted the couch cushion. Houston stepped over the line, quietly sitting close and wrapping his arm around her fragile shoulders. She reached for his hand, braiding their fingers.

"I *still* don't like you."

"Apology accepted."

Madison turned to him, searching his face for some kind of motive, deliberating his eyes and lips.

"*These* always get me in trouble."

She put her index finger on his lips and grabbed his shirt, pulling him closer until their noses almost touched. Houston traced her wounded face with his fingertips. His touch poetically complemented her pain.

Things Left Unspoken

Houston was in the kitchen when he heard Madison turn on the shower. The plumbing squealed as water hit the cold tile with thrust, changing tones when Madison moved into its force. Her bruised ribs rebelled against the water's rush and she turned her back, hailing a few choice obscenities. The cadence of the water drowned her weeping.

Madison shut off the water, letting it race down her body to the drain. Through the beveled shower glass, she saw Houston leaning against the door jamb. Madison reached for a towel, unable to hide her anguished eyes and nose when she finally opened the shower door to him.

Her clean skin pushed through Houston and into the bedroom. She retrieved the envelope she had found in the floor safe with Rhett's will. She fingered it, her mannerisms crisp and precise. She leered with caution at Houston, tossing the letter onto the unmade bed. Trust is an invisibly blatant, unassuming action they were ratifying.

Houston moved toward the letter. Madison stood watching the ocean out the window as it ebbed sluggishly at low tide. He caught Madison's stitched, scarred cheekbone commanding his peripheral vision.

M - Your father's name is Peck Fleming. He's a lawyer for my uncle's family. We are associated well with one another regarding everything. You are almost as good as your mother was at keeping secrets. You will know how to contact him when you destroy the kite. – Rhett

Tequila Sunset

The late October sunset that once fed Madison's denial now stifled it. The humidity from the storms suffocated her reasoning. She was a worm in hot ash, unable to calm the rampant anger in her belly. In the cabinet behind the aspirin sat a bottle of 1800 Tequila. She cracked the seal, smelling the sweet agave blend as she poured a shot into a small scotch glass and sipped it. It burned her lips, warm and enthralling.

192

Opera music boomed as she drank late into the evening darkness when she heard a car engine, then a single door slam. She turned down the music, lifting the blinds, making out Houston's chrome bumper in a distant neighbor's porch lights. He knocked on the door and she cracked it slightly, steadying her compromised stance in the dimly-lit room. Houston smelled tequila before she even ushered him inside. Her drunkenness was confirmed with the sweeping thud of the door.

"Drinking tequila tonight?"

"A little."

Houston turned on a lamp, examining the room. It was perfectly straight and tidy, nothing out of place. She poured some more tequila and handed him the glass. Houston swished the tequila around, sniffing it skeptically.

"What's behind those eyes tonight?"

"Just heavy things."

Madison turned up her glass, slamming it on the table with a grunt.

Houston felt the weightiness, suffocating heaviness in her volatile mood.

He built her a bonfire on the beach, hoping the velvety night sky would consume her unease. She was a powder keg. She sat guardedly close to him, sipping her tequila with resolve.

"I understand why you don't want to like me. Men frustrate and disappoint you."

Madison gave Houston a half sober, puzzled smirk. She chuckled, rubbing her temples smugly.

"Do you even know how to be a woman anymore?"

Madison threw her glass into the fire. She tossed the blanket off her shoulders, lunging at Houston. He restrained her wrists, watching her breasts bounce as she fought for control.

"*Woman* my ass - Rhett just handed me his balls and made me the man."

"Have you lived in the land of men so long that you just… put the balls on and wear them?"

Houston eventually released his grip, satisfied her conniption was corralled.

"I don't know *what* I am anymore."

He picked her up, carrying her inside, sand falling from every inch. Madison wrapped her arms around Houston's neck. Her felt her labored tequila breaths, her breasts pressed firmly against his chest.

Houston laid Madison onto the kitchen table, now dusted with sand. He groveled at the buttons on her blouse, giving up and ripping them off. He ran his hands up her stomach and over her breasts, finally tickling the nape of her neck with his whiskers.

"You feel like a woman…you even taste like a woman."

Madison kissed him so hard, taking his breath away only to abruptly push him aside and run out the door.

"Now you're *acting* like a woman."

Madison retched loud enough the neighbors turned on porch lights. Houston followed the sound, meeting her in the doorway as she stumbled into him.

"Maybe all I know how to do is vomit and fight?"

Houston put his arm around her fragile, half-naked torso, reaching for his shirt he had thrown in a chair. It smelled of his cologne and traces of tequila. Madison wore it half-buttoned. She was looking at the sandy kitchen table but her eyes appeared to have made it to China; they were distant, foreign. She organized the coarse grains into neat, symmetrical piles.

"I think I have made a mess of things."

"I think I like you when you drink tequila."

Madison smiled and the bruise on her cheek could have been mistaken for a blush. Houston reached for her hand and slipped her a small piece of paper.

"Call your father."

Diamond-sized tears sparkled in her jaded eyes. She watched Houston wrap his lips particularly around the rim of the tequila glass, remembering the feel of them parting into hers.

Peck Fleming

Madison worked the small piece of paper feverously between her fingers. It was light, paper thin yet was weighty with her anger and disdain. Her head buzzed from a hangover as she picked up the phone to dial.

"Peck Fleming."

He had a crisp, professional voice.

"Mr. Fleming. This is Madison Peacock."

His silence ebbed, molten lava.

"Rhett's been dead for almost three months. I thought I'd hear from you sooner… You did find Rhett's will?"

"Obviously, you drafted the will and knew Rhett well... everything well."

"Madison, you are the one that needs to know everything now. Vincent is using the money as a façade. He is staging a family takeover. It is annihilation for power. Rhett left you private financial accounts and

197

access to *everything*...I must deliver the family black book...It's not in the family vault."

"The vault still exists?"

"Mrs. Peacock, I know this has been difficult and you haven't been following the plan."

"How many times have you been following the *plan* having *known* I was your biological daughter?"

Peck found that her southern accent cradled her verbs nicely. She was brazen in a sincere way he instantly admired.

"You understood how Rhett worked, Mrs. Peacock. He separated the facts from the feelings. The facts are that Vincent was born with a condition that left him without fingerprints. Rhett changed the vault to fingerprint recognition. There has been a lot of recent activity to the vault... Just check the surveillance video."

"Why should I believe you? What do you have to gain?"

"You shouldn't...I just would put the innocent child foremost in your

plan…Use your feelings because anyone
that had that choice…well, they should."

Shadows have no voices or faces.
They are gray and influenced by the life they
trail, the life they are vested.

"How long had Rhett known about
Hannah?"

"Always, Mrs. Peacock…Rhett was
always a step ahead of his feelings."

The Intruder

Madison stared at the ceiling,
reliving the conversation two weeks ago she
had shared with Mr. Fleming. It had been
raining for a week straight, drowning out
Halloween trick or treating the prior
evening. Lightening signaled the thunder,
begetting the impending storm, striking with
a violent, echoing crack followed by thunder
in low baritone. It seemed to expand slowly,
inching dangerously closer.

Madison moved to the couch in the
darkness, lightening illuminated her path.
She massaged her overwrought eyes,

hearing the ocean waves hit violently into the shore. Lightning flickered multiple times, outlining a face pressing against the window, straining for sight. Madison recognized the prominent nostrils fogging up the glass. She flung open the door, ramming Lane's face into the carpet. Madison heaved her by her wet shirt, rolling her over and pinning her by the throat.

"What in the hell are you doing!?"

Lane choked, gasping for air, shaking her head from side to side, unable to speak. She screamed in raspy gasps.

"My family...They are gone."

"Hannah and Dyer?"

"Not *your* family...mine."

Madison turned on a light and Lane's sobs ceased. Lane noticed the scar on Madison's cheekbone.

"Shit - He beat you up?"

Madison began clapping her hands in sardonic applause, her bruised stomach still sore from Vincent's blows.

"You know what Vincent wants, Lane. You also know that I am the only one who can give it to him. You set your family up for him. He took them *all* out one by one. That is why you are playing both sides…playing me."

"At least I play… I don't hide from my true nature."

Lane moved close to Madison, eye to eye; she rubbed Madison's inner thigh, finding loaded cold steel.

"I know you, Madison. We connected."

Lane wound her fingers around Madison's hair, tipping her head slightly before kissing the ridge of her chin. Madison seized Lane's throat, ramming her into the door.

"I know you, too. Your whole greedy family tried the thumbprint reader at the vault. Everyone's declined…you and Hannah had no prints register."

Lane winced, but Madison only tightened her grip.

"Like father, like daughter."

Lane's eyes were crazed, frenzied. Lane rebutted, slapping Madison across her scar as she kneed Madison's tender ribcage. Madison curled to fetal position.

"*You* are Vincent's daughter."

A large, deafening roar emanated from the depths of Lane's very honest disgust. Her forehead wrinkled in anguish, her knuckles white as she shook. Lane's rage possessed her as she struck Madison repeatedly with her fists.

"It wasn't supposed to be like this! You bitch! I've kept Dyer and Hannah safe for you! I have *nothing* if I don't have you!"

Madison wailed loudly in pain and disappointment. Lane ended her genetic tirade, falling to the floor.

"Forgive me, forgive me…I'm so, so sorry, so sorry, so sorry…."

Lane stroked Madison's hair, petting her red face with trembling fingers.

"I do believe you love me, Lane. As much as I hate what you are doing right now, going through… I understand… I have always loved you. You are part of my family now. Your DNA betrays you. That is why I can't trust you...especially with Hannah's life."

Lane wrapped her skinny arms around Madison, cradling their dysfunction. She kissed the nape of Madison's neck, sniveling through her guilt. Lane brushed the cut on Madison's cheek, ashamed of her reaction. The two were very dangerous and potent, full of physical love and rage.

Broken Shells

Houston checked his wrist watch, noticing Madison was late for their beach walk. He looked warily to Lane's BMW under her carport. History was shady regarding this friend. He put his hands to the glass door, cutting the glare so he could see inside. He tried the knob, but it was locked. He reached above the door frame, toying with the extra key, his instincts quarreling. He stared at the red key for a long moment before sliding it into the lock.

There was stirring in the bedroom as Madison dressed. Houston roved the curvature of her strong back as she slid her arms through the sleeves of her t-shirt. She mothered Lane, patting her dark hair to one side as she slept, her naked arms and legs tangled through the sheets. Madison's scar appeared irritated, fresh in the sun lit window. Houston cleared his throat, startling Madison. The fine lines on her forehead were filled with a duty he couldn't fathom. She limped to him.

"I'm sorry. I'm late."

He laced his fingers through hers, kissing her newly cut and bruised knuckles. His eyes danced from wound to wound. Houston quietly closed the door to the boardwalk and Lane's eyes opened.

"I see your friend has finished what she started."

Houston noticed the pallor of Madison's skin as she faced the sun. It cast her expression silvery and sad.

"I got her where I need her…and I wouldn't call her a friend. She's my family."

Madison curled her arms across her sore stomach.

She kicked over a shell, disappointed in its holes. The sand had hidden its brokenness. Houston bent down, picking up the shell she had shunned. She saw him put it in his pocket.

"Why do you keep doing that...pocketing the broken ones?"

Houston's eyes were gray as dusk, his energy tall and commanding as he towered over Madison. He reached back in his pocket, pulling out the shell and placing it in Madison's palm.

"Sometimes the broken ones are the most challenging."

"God, I still don't like you."

Madison bounced the shell off his nose. He cinched her arm, forcing it behind her back. The scent of her skin was sensually clean and imposing. Her body fought her eyes' intentions.

Madison laid her cheek on his chest. He ran his hands over her hips rather hypnotically, working his way up her back.

Madison nibbled his lower lip. They began swapping avid kisses and her knees buckled, sending them passionately into the sand.

Lane watched Madison's intimacy from the bedroom window as she dialed.

"It's me. She has found the book."

She cringed. She continued to watch them kissing, jealously gritting her teeth.

A Little Trust

Lane smoked a cigarette, perched on the steps of Madison's deck. She flicked the ash glibly, watching Madison return from her jaunt with Houston. Lane sized Madison up, blowing smoke high into the air. Madison sat near Lane, brushing sand from her clothes.

"How is Hannah?"

"They are having a hell of a time…and why wouldn't they…we just pulled them into our craziness."

"Hence my distance."

Lane spied Houston moving further up the beach, talking on his phone.

"What are you doing, Madison? You playing house with him?"

"We're *friends*. That's all you get."

"Don't fool yourself, no one understands our lives…and if you kiss all your *friends* like that then there is hope for me."

She reached into the pocket on her oversized shirt, pulling out a prepaid cell phone. She handed it to Madison.

"Call *our* family."

Lane put her cigarette out on the wooden deck before flinging it into the sand. She disappeared down the boardwalk, walking in the opposite direction of Houston's approach.

Houston sported a bottle of chardonnay across his shoulder like a baseball bat. He offered it to Madison as she stared at the cell phone Lane had just given her. She debated, challenging her love and her intellect.

"I don't know how to trust anyone."

Madison rubbed the phone over and over with her index finger. He noticed her searching periodically, keeping Lane in view.

"You can learn to trust again…but it is different."

"I want to - I'm not ready to forget."

He opened the screw top bottle of wine and took a drink straight from the bottle.

"Everything is *secure* for your trip back to Little Rock."

He took another drink, licking his lips.

"Isn't it a little early for wine…like eight hours."

He handed the bottle to her with duress. She cocked her head back as she turned the bottle skyward, taking a large gulp.

"That was sage of you, woman. I think you just trusted me."

Madison grinned mischievously, and he admired her smile lines that worked their marking into her cheeks. She flipped the cell phone open, looking to him for approval. He saluted her. She dialed.

"Hannah Beth, it's Momma…Yes, I'm coming home."

Section V

Back to Life

November 2007

The trees were a palate of orange and
red dotting the Arkansas skyline as
Madison's plane descended into Little Rock.
It was the week before Thanksgiving and the
colors were in full fall splendor. Arkansas
looked so peaceful, so artistic from a pilot's
view. Madison sighed as the plane touched
down with a thud. Somehow this was
harder, more difficult than she had
imagined. Madison was different, more
calculated and put together.

As she deplaned and walked to the
breezeway, she felt place, time, season; the
air was spicy with death, renewal. The
beach was without place or time, a vortex of
memory and mood. Madison understood its
safety, its allure. Her mania hadn't been
quelled with the routine rhythms of the
ocean and the tides. Leaves blew about,
hard and crisp, grating against the concrete,
screeching their sonnet to the wind.
Madison watched them dance and swirl,

finding her steps strange and catlike on the pavement. The sand had made her concentrate on her balance, her posture, aware of herself, her surroundings; the concrete had given her a false sense of stability, leaving her vulnerable, easily tripped. Madison felt taller, even though the world was more menacing.

She was staying at the newly-renovated Capitol Hotel. She loved the River Market during change of seasons. There were always activities moving people about in celebration; the Natural State lined with beauty. On the cab ride to the hotel, Madison realized this would be her first holiday truly alone. Her mother and her husband were now both gone.

Once unpacked and settled into her room, she took a walk down through the storefronts of the River Market district. The sun was beginning to set and Madison found a park bench along the scenic walking path. A barge pushed along the Arkansas River on this very vivid, unseasonably warm November evening. Madison watched people, studied their expressions, and imagined their lives. Some smiled at her, noticing her gaze. She blended in nicely with the crowd, just another passerby.

The sun left golden rays in its goodbye, highlighting the intricate cobwebs woven with precision and care by frenzied spiders. In the distance, a shadow watched her. She could only make out the silhouette of a tall, stocky man puffing on a cigarette. He stomped out the cigarette with his shoe and turned and walked in the opposite direction. She wondered how many webs her frenzied spider had awaiting her. Amidst the children's shrieks and the low hum of the barge, she felt little pieces of her heart changing like the leaves around her.

She had returned at dusk, sipping tequila, crying softly as she watched the foot traffic below from her window. She changed clothes, rifling through her bag, looking for the shirt of Houston's she had snuck into her suitcase. As she slipped it around her naked shoulders and breasts, she felt something in the shirt pocket. Madison wiped her bleary eyes with the sleeve and reached for the strange object. It was an empty airplane bottle of tequila. Madison's tears turned to laughter. Inside was a rolled up piece of paper. It read 911 dial 1-777-HOU-KING. It was Houston's private cell number. She dialed and he heard her muffled sobs at the other end.

"You've been drinking tequila?"

"I turn forty tomorrow."

Madison played with the dress buttons on his shirt, staring down at the scarce city street activity.

"That's NOT why you are drinking tequila."

Houston was admiring the full moon from his deck, listening to the waves.

"I'm afraid. I don't know how to be a mother...what if I am terrible?"

Madison bawled into his shirt collar.

"Hannah picked you for the job. You've been her mother, can't you see? Besides, I knew the moment I first saw you flying that kite that you were fearless."

"Alone at the beach maybe…this place makes me crazy."

Houston heard Madison's pleas in her angry outbursts, drunken tirades, and snotty tears.

"You have to know…I think…I think I'm in *like* with you."

Horns beeped in the distance as Madison sighed deeply into the receiver.

"You're plain beautiful drinking tequila. It makes you honest."

Houston was certain Madison was the woman worth the risk.

Synergy

Madison finally drifted off, rolling her past before her like an old movie reel. She had lived a very intense, extreme existence the past ten years. She listened to the clicks of the film as it flickered brilliantly in her mind until the film finally ran out, clapping loudly with Rhett's gunshot. Nausea and chills made a nasty combination.

Madison's phone beeped, startling her. She opened her text message groggily, still half asleep.

Dyer: Welcome home, stranger.

Madison replied as her fingertips rebelled against the tequila.

Madison: Missed u. Howz Hannah?

Unwarranted guilt crept up her torso. Madison rolled over onto her back, staring at the street lights angled on the ceiling. She had brought Hannah a mason jar of shells she had collected each day at the beach. Nostalgia filled her heart: sadness made it sink to her toes.

Dyer: OK

Madison rubbed her temples, closing her eyes, feeling adrenaline throbbing madly through her blood.

Madison: Need to see you both. Staying @ the Capitol # 1252. Meet @ 11 tomorrow?

Dyer: OK...the spiderz everywhere

Madison opened the heavy solid door to Dyer and his cologne washed over her face. She could smell his skin and, in a very primal way, her heart began to beat with their shared agenda. Dyer's hair was longer, his face stubble more pronounced. He was wearing a crisp white button-down shirt, jeans, a black leather jacket and black cowboy boots. Dyer was handsome in a rugged sense. He smiled his usual, easy half-grin. They both stood, taking a long look at the other, finding their synergy was still present.

Madison extended her arms to hug Dyer as reserve bounced between them. Their mannerisms were divisive as their bodies touched slightly, respecting the new unmentionables that had entered their lives. Dyer kissed Madison respectfully on the cheek. Madison's arms fell away first.

"Where's Hannah?"

"She's with a friend in the lobby. I wanted to talk with you first."

They sat on the couch side by side and Dyer noticed the vivid scar on Madison's face. He reached for it in concern and she turned her face away in shame.

"He's getting into Hannah's head. She won't talk to me about it. Just keeps talking about the spider. I don't know what else to do. This is getting serious."

Madison walked to the window, staring out into the blue November sky. Her sobs echoed off the high ceiling of the room and bounced like a ball from corner to corner

"Madison, what happened on that beach?"

Madison turned to him, her eyes bleak and sorrowful. He stared at her scar.

"There is so much I want to tell you. I don't like hiding things from you."

Madison sat close to Dyer once again, putting her hand on his knee as he stared at the floor.

"We are so good together when it comes to Hannah Beth."

He moved his hand to hers, massaging her index finger and thumb with his own callused ones.

"Vincent is Lane's biological father. What he did to me on the beach is only a warm up for the rest of us."

Loud pounding on the door, followed by Hannah Beth's shrill hollers, interrupted their intensity. They both raced to the door to find Hannah with her hands on her hips, tears welling in her eyes. Dyer and his friend, a young woman, shared an affectionate gaze before she walked in the direction of the elevator. Hannah grabbed Madison's hand, pulling her down to her level. She kissed Madison repeatedly, placing her tiny trembling hands on Madison's cheeks.

"What took you so long?!"

There was frenzy in Hannah's temper that worried Madison.

"Your daddy says you've been seeing the spider. Tell me what he says to scare you."

Hannah hesitated, picking her purple nail polish, looking to Dyer then back to Madison.

"I can't tell you."

221

"Hannah, when you let the fear in, it swallows you. When you tell on it, it disappears."

"Not this spider. He crawls out of everything and tells me gross, icky stories. He tells me if I'm not good that bad things will happen."

"What does he tell you so gross and frightening?"

Hannah looked to Madison and then to Dyer in contemplation.

"That you won't be my momma and that you won't be my daddy. That you will die and I will have to live with him."

"We are raising you. We aren't dying. Why didn't you tell your daddy this?"

"He said if I told one of you, it would come true."

Hannah's lips quivered, magnifying her starry blue eyes. Madison held Hannah close as she cried into her chest.

"Whatever it takes, Hannah Beth. We're going to protect you."

"But…How do I protect *you*?"

Hannah carried the weightiness of guilt in her tiny world. Dyer and Madison exchanged tearful glances. Dyer moved in closer, rubbing Hannah's tiny shoulders with his strong hands.

Happy Birthday

"What time do you want me to pick you up for your birthday dinner tonight?"

Madison heard the roar of Lane's BMW through the phone. Lane was now living in Little Rock. She had purchased Rhett's lucrative law practice from Madison.

"Who said anything about dinner?"

"You only turn forty once."

"I'm not in the mood, Lane."

"Wear something black, pearls, pumps. Be ready by seven."

Lane grimaced as she lied, whipping the car into the turning line at the hotel. The BMW idled like a purring kitten. Her passenger got out of the car after she threw Madison's room key at him, peeling out of the parking lot.

The birthday bottle of Patron Silver tequila sat on the edge of the bathtub with a shot glass. Madison lit a candle in celebration as she ran a very, very hot bath that steamed up the mirrors. She had bought some fresh verbena bubble bath down at a little store she had frequented in her other life. Low music played on her clock radio and she turned out all the lights except for one by the bed and the candle burning in her bathroom. The flames danced off the tile in a mesmerizing pace to the music.

Madison threw her bra and panties onto the floor, pouring a shot of tequila as she eased painfully into the sauna she had created. She raised her glass, toasting *Happy Birthday* under her breath, sipping the tequila. Madison followed the warmth down her throat as it soothed her fears in its descent. When it hit her stomach, it flopped like a fish out of water, dancing on her nerves. She drank the remainder of the shot, slamming the glass on the side of the tub with a sigh.

She put her face in her hands, smearing her makeup, sobbing in privacy. Madison thought of her day with Dyer. They were both trying to save the innocence of a little girl that only wanted a family. Madison had once had the same plight as Hannah, growing up without a father. She cried for all Hannah had endured and for what lay ahead. The stress that all the men in her life had inflicted bubbled to the top.

Madison was finishing up her makeup, preparing for a dinner she was dreading when the phone rang.

"You ready?"

"Come on up. Use your key."

Madison was zipping her dress when the door opened. Lane never spoke, but Madison could hear her moving around the room, finding a seat. Madison slipped her pumps on as she fastened her pearls, walking to meet the person she thought was Lane.

"I hope you're happy. I'm wearing pumps and pearls."

"Happy birthday."

Madison froze as she rounded the corner into the bedroom.

He sat in the easy chair, dressed in a sports coat and Armani shirt.

"That lying bitch…You know we had an agreement."

"You can't turn forty alone."

Houston's eyes roved her body approvingly. Her fair skin shimmered in the black dress.

Houston had reserved a private room. In the middle of the table was a bottle of tequila with two glasses. He did the honors as Madison watched him, wondering about his agenda.

"How was your visit with Dyer and Hannah?"

"Vincent is brainwashing my six-year-old with fear…I don't want to talk about that."

Madison crossed her arms, furling her nose in frustration.

"You can't control this situation. You have to stick to the plan."

"I just want to protect them. I just *feel* too much."

Madison poured more tequila into her glass. She took a long drink, closing her eyes. Houston could practically see the vapor trails as she exhaled. The filet mignon arrived. She picked at her food silently as they ate, lost in a spiral of guilt and regret that was taking her under.

Houston corked the bottle of tequila and offered his arm in escort.

Sway and Sand

Madison made it back to her room rather clumsily. Houston steadied her as she unlocked the door. The sound of jazz horn greeted them as they entered a dark, candle lit room. The scents from Madison's bath danced about the air, adding to the mystique. On the dining table by the window sat the challenge. Sand was strewn all over it and Madison's birthday bottle of Patron tequila with two shot glasses. Houston was standing behind Madison, guiding her by her shoulders when she noticed the setup. He felt her shudder, getting weak, sliding a bit.

Houston led her to the middle of the room, took her in his arms and began swaying side to side, dipping her slowly, kissing the nape of her neck. Houston felt Madison's body wavering. He put his hand behind the small of her back as they rocked side to side with the low, sultry music. He ran his fingers over her breasts and shoulders, and finally down to the small of her back.

Houston unzipped Madison's dress, pulling it from her shoulders and letting it drop to the floor. Madison closed her eyes as Houston led with his lips. She retraced their conversations on the beach. She swam in his eyes. He hadn't been an instant rush but a slow burning ember, now so very controlled and hot. She let his hands roam private places she denied other men.

He shoved her onto the sandy table, grabbing the bottle of tequila. He pulled the cork off with his teeth, taking a long drink before generously pouring it on Madison's stomach and breasts. She rubbed her hands through the expensive tequila now oozing down her torso and he suckled each finger one by one, burning his tongue and lips. His tongue chased the tequila that had run down her thighs and between her legs.

The wind cares nothing about how beautiful or sturdy the kite, but rather the driving skill of the man pulling on all the strings.

Rainy Day Mantras

The starry night gave into the thick, billowy storm clouds of early dawn. The morning cried, running the fall colors into a muted gray. Houston stood in the window, wearing only his khaki's, his hands in his pockets. His mind rode on the back of the raindrops, as he basked in the unspoken lover's afterglow. He watched Madison sleep. She was tangled in a sheet, her mouth wide open as she snored lightly. Her very original, intimate moans were audible again in the silent walls of his memory. His hands had memorized the feel of her body, absorbing her chemistry. He held his hands to his nose. He could smell her skin on his. He wondered what she was dreaming now.

Madison stirred, speaking with her delicate smile. She ran her fingers through her unkempt hair, examining her nakedness protruding in opportune places. She coveted Houston's strong arms, posed in tender interrogation. His eyes were gray, reflecting the morning monotone out the window. He sat on the bed, running his hand over her curves; her perceived imperfections no longer an issue. Madison rose up on her elbows, finding his slow heat satisfying. She felt something cold upon her chest. She grabbed at it, finding a charm on the end of a necklace. On the end of a long, rope chain was a kite charm with a diamond stud in the middle. Madison kissed the charm, swallowing the large lump in her throat.

They lay close, listening to the rain flood the window and run down the panes.

He could feel her heart beating thunderously as she fidgeted with the new charm, rolling it nervously in her fingers. Ominous thunder rumbled in the late November morning. Lightning awakened the gloom. Madison turned to Houston with the eyes of a child. She wrapped herself in Houston's dress shirt and walked to the window, paying homage to the lightning and thunder. Two lovers holding hands ran across the street against the rain.

"Last night…something changed…"

"You trust yourself."

Houston held out his hand to her. She hesitated, staring at his fingertips wiggling, her lifeline if she chose to accept. Madison dove from the exiled cliff she had built over the years; falling deeply, her fingers firmly entangled in Houston's resilient grip.

Puzzle Pieces

Madison's glasses rested low on her nose as she read the contents of the *Bianchi* folder Houston had given her. She held the documents in her right hand as she methodically balled her left hand into a fist, extending her fingers then back to a fist.

Madison turned the old style faucet heads fluidly; the water resounded off the smooth refinished bathtub. There was a storm brewing; the air was thick and heavy. She turned around and reached for her coffee on the countertop and a gloved hand snatched her wrist, pulling her into the other room. She moved very calmly, her eyes a raging tornado.

They stood face to face. Vincent tossed the file she had been reading high into the air and it littered the room in white.

"So ya think ya know everythin' now?"

Vincent reached into his coat, pulling out half of the black book he had stolen from Rhett.

"My husband left *me* to be the thorn in your side. You need me for more than the other half of the book and we both know it…"

He swung the book at Madison and she ducked, kicking him in the shin. He cursed inaudible obscenities.

"Once you get your hands on the other half of this book, I'm comin' at ya. I slaughtered my whole greedy family for the contents of the vault…and you're goin' to open that safe for me."

She fingered the cold steel handgun she had strapped on her inner thigh, contemplating pointing it at his brow.

"I'd shoot you right now if I could…"

"But ya can't 'cause you're just a dirty little snake wrapped in a pretty package… who knows it's a game of timin'."

Vincent charged Madison, plowing her onto the couch and into the sea of strewn papers. His gloved hand pinned her in a choke hold.

"Are you fast enough to save them all? I think I'll let ya live, kill everyone else and make ya watch. Hannah would watch, too…before I snapped her neck right in front of ya."

Madison spit in his eyes, punching him in his windpipe.

Vincent barreled out of Madison's room, knocking pictures off the wall in his raging helplessness.

Surprises

Madison removed her spike heels as the helicopter hummed louder and louder on approach. Houston had chartered it for an evening flight over the river.

"If I had known about this, I would have worn real shoes and pants."

"Did you forget how to be a lady while playing with all those boys?"

Madison flipped him the bird haughtily. She handed him her heels, hiking her dress a few inches as she climbed into the copter. Houston gave her a push, feeling the shiny steel gun affixed to her lean leg. She continually surprised him. The sunset flight flew over the holiday lighted state

234

capital. The city was small, cozy even from above. The full moon haunted Madison with its blue and silvery tones. The streets were quiet with a small town silence as if the roads had been rolled up after midnight. The stars faint midnight freckles. A barge whistle bellowed from the moonlit river as fog began to form around the street lamps and pillars. Madison laid her head on his shoulder as they watched the sun fall into the river, both missing the ocean's seclusion.

A limo shuttled them back to the Capitol Hotel where a concierge ushered them to a private stairwell. Houston had reserved an entire ballroom of the hotel, complete with a jazz band. Low music emanated and Madison's blood slowed to the sound. Houston slid a hand to the small of her back before opening the door and she moaned discernibly.

The room was dimly lit with freshly polished hardwood floors, and the small band lent closeness to the grand corners. The large picture windows lined the north wall, the front of the hotel, the starry night part of their scenery. In front of the window was a single, solitary table for two. A liquid black baby grand piano was the central, most romantic instrument in the room. The band faded into a sultry saxophone. Houston threaded his fingers through Madison's, pulling her close, wanting to feel her against him as they danced. Her body never lied. It was unyielding tonight. When the song ended, he guided her to their table where the champagne was chilling. Madison looked out the window at the full moon as it cast foreboding on the room. She had steel walls around her. Houston poured champagne. He reached for her hand, now an unconscious fist. He unrolled its rigidity, massaging her fingernails. They sipped champagne, finding the music an ingenious distraction.

"You read people well, Madison. You handled Vincent today with a bag of balls like I've never seen in a woman."

Madison's mouth fell agape in shock. She batted her eyes in astonishment.

"How'd you...I didn't tell you..."

Houston stroked the kite charm necklace balanced between her breasts.

"Wear this always, stubborn woman."

"You bugged *me*?"

Her voice boomed with sexy anger.

"I love you, let me protect you."

He glared at the scar on her cheekbone and she reached for his hand, kissing his palm. She rolled the kite charm with her thumb and forefinger as tears streamed down her crooked grin.

The band had left and the room was cleared. An empty champagne bottle lay on the table as another bottle sat on ice. Houston walked to the lonely piano and filled their glasses with the final champagne. He sat on the bench and began playing a song. Madison watched his fingers move fluidly across the keys as she sat close to him. He closed his eyes, pecking an unfamiliar saucy tune. He reiterated certain sensual chords, teasing her interest.

Madison lifted her skirt, straddling him on the bench, halting his opus. She bit his lower lip, aggressively pulling at his shirttails. Her alcohol-slowed fingers dueled with her urgency. Her method was raw and present. He kissed her breasts through the low plunge of her neckline. His hands disappeared under her cinched dress. Houston's touch traced the handgun's strapping, salaciously tickling her inner thighs. She roared shamelessly.

"Oh, God...I...I love you."

Houston hiked the hem of Madison's dress to her waist, propping her on the piano keys as he moved into her. She threw her head back, banging out mismatched notes of ebony and ivory, the piano now trumpeting her feelings. The keys jangled oddly to the rhythm of their sex, their love now an off-key symphony.

They donned mismatched pieces of their clothing like fig leaves, sitting close enough their shoulders touched. Their intimacies had locked horns at times, making the passion avid and raging, tender and brusque. Madison put her hand on his bare knee. Houston ran his fingers across the piano keys before closing the cover that crashed with a thud. Its echo sobered them for the task ahead. They braided their jaded fingers into one convincing grip.

Timing

The smell of soap awakened Madison. Houston could be heard moving around the bathroom. His long strides were evident even in a small space. She tried to fathom how simplicity such as his had become meshed into her every day. Houston fit well.

Madison smelled his cologne getting stronger. She didn't move, feigning sleep. Houston sat beside her on the bed, watching her eyelids jerk. She savored memories of their evening as her back ached from the piano keys.

"Come on, tough girl, time to get dressed."

"What does a tough girl wear in a kill or be killed situation?"

"You use sarcasm when you are crying inside."

Madison opened her eyes. He caressed her high, soft cheekbone, admiring her lazy grin. Houston's hand was warm, spicy. Madison kissed his palm, reaching for his shirt collar, pulling herself into his personal space. The champagne had dehydrated her, made her listless.

"I just have a bad feeling."

"Just stick to the plan."

He leaned in to kiss Madison, her eyes a sea of distress. He felt her fears heckling her with doubt. Houston's eyes were turquoise. His mouth upturned slightly as he looked to Madison, showing small glints of his lust.

"I love you Madison – good and bad."

They consumed the seconds, passing those nuggets of encouragement. Houston caressed her breast, slipping a lock box key in her cleavage.

"How did you get inside of me?"

"I just crawled in through that hole in your chest."

Park Bench Conversations

Holiday wishes and signs were being put up in the River Market district. It was a few days before Thanksgiving. The wind blew the debris into mini-tornados, colorfully dancing from street to sidewalk. Madison buttoned her coat as she watched nature's display.

She flipped up her coat collar this particularly bright, windy November mid-morning. Each step through the River Market was against the wind, blowing her hair about wildly, speaking to her with its force, encouraging her toward her fate. Peck Fleming sat on the bench facing the river, his back to Madison and his face in profile. She stopped ten feet away, examining him. He was tall and slender with a thick head of white and silver hair, wavy around the temples like hers. From the profile, Madison could tell she had his very definite nose. It seemed larger on him. She walked to the bench, her hands in her coat pockets.

"Good morning, Mr. Fleming."

"Madison."

He patted the bench, offering her a seat next to him, never looking into her eyes. He appeared physically fit for his seventy-two years. Madison joined him. Her stomach ached. This was the first time she had sat beside someone with her same genes in years. She had always wondered what it would have been like as a child to walk or play in the park with her father. When Peck addressed Madison, he noticed she smiled like her mother.

"Mr. Fleming, I don't have much time. First, I am not Rhett. I am very aware of how to connect the facts and my emotions without drowning in the mix."

"I understand."

"When the facts don't feel right, I don't trust anyone. I know how I want to feel toward you, your intentions seem
242

genuine. But in this case putting feelings ahead of facts is dangerous when it threatens a child."

"I am still a complete stranger regardless of the DNA. I haven't given you a reason to trust me. Nothing is as it seems as you've discovered. I assume you read the folder I sent?"

"I am the fingerprint code to the vault."

She reached in her coat pocket, pulling out a picture of Hannah.

"This plan is a dead man's. Here is the reason we are doing *this* plan *my* way. Everyone involved or tied to this has their own agendas. This is the only one that matters."

Peck held the photo with his long, slender fingers.

"Please help me protect her, Mr. Fleming. I think I have found a fool-proof way."

Peck stared at the picture of Hannah, then locked eyes with the daughter he hadn't known existed, hoping this wasn't the first

243

and last time. Barge whistles bellowed. A smaller boat zipped past, its motor wound out at a high pitch. The wind blew leaves to their feet, swirling them around their shoes, clinging like the shadows in the distance.

Lane Changes

Lane knocked weakly on Madison's door before entering. She greeted Madison with a weary, despondent glare. Madison had been reviewing her revised will that now sat on the couch alongside her handgun. Her hair was still a bit damp around the ends, highlighting her haste. Madison caught Lane's eyes roving the obvious remnants of her romance with Houston, noticing their clothes from the previous evening strewn intermittently across the room. Madison reached for her handgun as she put her will back in her briefcase.

"You remember how to use this, right?"

"Oh, yeah."

Madison loaded the clip swiftly, cocking the gun, loading the first bullet into the chamber. Lane grinned slyly in cheer, turned on by Madison's command of the weapon. She imagined unloading the whole clip on Vincent.

"You know what to do, Lane. Please, do it this time."

Madison forced the gun into Lane's hand.

"Maybe one day... I won't remind you of all the bad...Madison - promise me that?"

Madison locked her fingers around Lane's limp grip on the gun.

The Slip Up

Lane had called Vincent, letting him know Madison was to get the black book today. It was now a game of precision and proximity. Dyer had decided to take Hannah to a crowded, public children's arts festival where it would be more difficult for a gruff, imposing man to blend in. Dyer had seen

Vincent skulking all morning, unable to snatch Hannah. Lane and Madison split up once they arrived at the River Market Pavilion. Lane spotted Dyer drinking coffee. She approached Dyer, nodding to him to follow, but he shook his head, thwarting the plan. He turned his back to Lane and, puzzled, she took the signal, and left.

Madison searched for Hannah, who was finger painting. She sneaked behind Hannah, pulling her pigtail. Hannah shrieked with excitement, hugging Madison, showing her the picture she had just created. Madison whispered in Hannah's ear and took her hand. She knew Hannah would go anywhere with her. Lane had parked nearby. Madison's heart hit her feet when she saw Lane standing alone by her car. Lane flailed her hands in frustration as Madison cursed her with her eyes.

Lane drove downtown with Madison and Hannah. They entered a private garage two blocks away where another car awaited to take Lane and Hannah anonymously through a back entrance to the vault building. Madison took Lane's car, parking in front of the vault building. She entered, finding the room with lockboxes, using the key Houston had given her to open box 12 where she found the other half of the black book.

Lane led Madison and Hannah to the vault. The vault was more like a small apartment. It was temperature controlled with ventilation. Rhett had spent many a night here, archiving the Godair family's business. It was a veritable goldmine for a crook like Vincent. The vault accepted Madison's fingerprint. Hannah clapped. Madison put the black book on a shelf with other similar looking ones before kissing Hannah then locking Lane and Hannah safely in its steel confines.

Madison revved Lane's car engine as she locked the doors and dialed her voicemail.

"Madison, I'm sorry I couldn't go along with your plan. I can't make promises when it threatens your safety. Go back to your hotel room."

Dyer had been the monkey wrench in their plan, sacrificing himself.

The Barter

Madison parked Lane's car and walked to the hotel, her own shadow threatening. She slid her key into the door of her room, hearing the familiar click. She crept through the darkness, hearing Dyer's labored breaths. The cold steel of Vincent's knife pressed against Madison's neck. Vincent grabbed Madison's fine hair, yanking her into his face. His breath was fowl as garbage. Madison tried kicking him between the legs, but he whacked her across the face. A slow trickle of blood ran out of her nose, climbing the mountains of her lips before exiting her chin. The sound of the blood drop hitting the ground was almost audible.

Vincent pushed Madison into Dyer, turning on a lamp. Dyer was almost unrecognizable, his face black and blue as he sat bound on the couch. White papers

248

from Madison's will were littered all around him, some sticking to his bloody skin.

"I saw your new will. Did ya think you could keep Hannah alive by givin' her all *my* money?"

He girded rope viciously around her wrists and ankles.

"Did ya know Lane traded one family for another? Yea…she bartered her whole inheritance to save your ass. Makes ya kinda sick, don't it."

He took their cell phones and put them in his pocket before turning off the lamp. Vincent slammed them back into the semi-darkness.

Tough Girl

Madison studied each wound on Dyer's face, aware of death's proximity. Dyer opened his swollen eyes, hearing Madison whimpering a tragedy.

"Madison, are they safe?"

"Yes…you… and Lane…you sacrificed *everything*. Why?"

"Everything is nothing without you and Hannah."

"Vincent is right, you know. We've all traded one family for another...we're all family now, Dyer."

"Maybe we'll all get it right this time?"

Dyer would always love Madison for never giving up on their dream of raising Hannah.

Dyer began floating in and out of consciousness, at times speaking in a tongue Madison couldn't understand. She listened intently to his rhythmic huffs, worrying about his injuries as more time passed. Minutes seemed like hours in the blackness of seclusion. Madison bowed her head in anguish when her chin grazed the charm around her neck.

"I know you can hear me...I hope you have your doctor friend near because we are both going to need her...if we make it... Dyer is a mess...please be careful...'cause this tough girl...well...she needs you...she loves you."

Through the hum of the air conditioning unit, Madison thought she heard three soft, purposeful taps on the wall, emanating from the room next door.

Powerless Torture

Vincent sounded like a bull bursting through the door. Whiskey wafted into Madison's face. He was smoking a cigar as he staggered a bit, walking into the dark room. He turned the lamp back on, swiftly slapping Madison with the back of his hand, belching obscenely. Madison dropped her head, grunting from the numbing sting of his ring.

Dyer bucked in his chair. His marred eyes seethed fury. Vincent realized just how much power he had over them. He hit one and the other winced in sympathy. Vincent fed on their fear. He blew smoke in Dyer's black and blue eyes.

"You'd give your left nut to save her, hurts to see her in pieces."

Vincent cupped Madison's left breast, roaming Madison's torso and resting his hand between her legs. The vein on Dyer's temple pulsated.

"What's the matter lover boy? Don't like me touchin' her?"

Dyer struggled against the ropes, his chair toppled on its side. His growl turned to a low, guttural moan.

Vincent fumbled in his jacket, pulling out a revolver. He pulled the hammer back, sticking the barrel to Dyer's temple, his finger nursing the trigger.

"You sure she's still worth it?"

He turned his contempt to Madison, pointing the gun between her crystal blue eyes. Vincent was enjoying this round of torture, compliments of the whiskey.

"You'd die for this waste of sperm? I'm so disappointed."

"What are you waiting for…you coward?"

Beads of sweat had formed on Vincent's forehead. Madison had blood

running down her mouth and neck, flowing
like the tears of her life.

"Let's open that vault."

Vincent and Madison locked eyes as
the end of the gun barrel kissed the bridge of
Madison's brow. He thrust the gun to
Dyer's temple execution style.

"Dyer goes."

Vincent hesitated as sweat poured
profusely from his bald head. He put the
gun back in his jacket. He untied Dyer from
the chair, his hand tightly bound as they
walked unnoticed through a private stairwell
to a parked car in the alley.

"Well, Vincent...I guess torture
really is for the powerless."

Madison scowled as her maimed
beauty ridiculed his murderous anxiety. He
forced her into the trunk alongside Dyer.

Dyer and Madison lay facing each
other. Madison stroked Dyer's swollen eyes.
Her nimble, bruised fingers eased the agony
while passing along little goodbyes. She
kissed his bulbous cheek, tasting his blood

on her lips, their DNA mixing, tasting bitter
and foul.

A Safe Bet

It was the day before Thanksgiving
and people were leaving work and rushing
around doing last minute errands. An
elderly woman carried a bag of groceries
and a young man toted her large turkey on
his shoulder as the car made its way
downtown to the vault. Madison listened to
the hum of the road as she worked to loosen
the ropes that Vincent had so tightly bound
around Dyer's wrists.

Dusk lent grayness to their shadows
as they meandered down a back alley at
gunpoint and into the back entrance of the
building. Vincent's men locked the door,
scurrying into the shadows.

Their mismatched footsteps echoed
off the polished tile floor as they walked the
long corridor to the vault. The silence was
haunting. Dyer stood directly behind
Madison. He could smell her skin, his heavy

254

breaths tangible. Madison's anger gave her body chemistry a sweet aroma that intoxicated Dyer's sanity, their rage synced and ready to kill.

Worry rushed through Vincent's veins; his hands shook as he unlocked the door to the vault room. Vincent throttled the doorknob, strong arming Madison to the safe. Dyer worked his hands free as Madison raised her bruised finger to the scanner. The gears to the lock on the safe released with a deep thump. The door lumbered open as a child's voice sobbed from inside.

Hannah poked her head around the vault door, searching for her mother. Madison opened her arms as her daughter dashed into her badly bruised chest. Madison knew the only safe place for Hannah was the one place Vincent's DNA could never access. Deceit burned Vincent's cheeks shades of crimson. Madison was a formidable foe, but he hadn't sold his soul for naught. He cursed a string of verbal diarrhea, never hearing the subtle squeaking

of the door hinges. Houston choked
Vincent's thick neck as Vincent engaged the
clip to his gun. Dyer stumbled toward
Madison as Vincent shot her in the back,
furtively unloading his clip. He peppered
the room with bullets, finally succumbing to
the revolver Houston jammed under his
meaty chin. Dyer had been hit while
blanketing Madison and Hannah. All three
lie motionless on the floor. The echo of the
bullets was deafening. The aftershock
buzzed in their now silent ears.

Hours of anxious pause had eroded
in mere milliseconds.
Lane kicked the vault door open, aiming
Madison's pistol at Vincent. Redemption
commanded her grip on the gun. Lane's
brown eyes teemed with the darkness she
had inherited from him. She searched
Vincent's face for something tenable before
firing twice, striking Vincent's kneecaps.
He buckled like a buffalo, falling to the floor
as Houston's stature dominated him.
Vincent's black blood ran freely, merging
with Madison's and Dyer's.

"You will always be attached to me, Lane. Just look in the goddamn mirror! There ain't a damn thing you can do about your DNA."

His breathing was labored and laced with his boorish hatred; His soul a cemetery of the pungent rot he fed upon.

Out of Lane's periphery, she noticed Hannah's small starry blue eyes peering up from under the rubble of bodies, blood pooled near Hannah's cheek. She was still wrapped in Madison's arms. Madison opened her fatigued eyes, looking to Lane. She cupped her bloody hand over Hannah's gaze.

"You're right. I can't choose my DNA."

Lane fired twice into Vincent's chest, leaving a gaping hole where a heart should be.

"But I can choose my family."

Epilogue
October 2013

The beach in October was so beautiful, the skies indigo with wispy, thin clouds hinting the cooler air. This seemed a fitting destination for his memorial. It was the place Madison had gotten to know him five years ago. They had walked hand in hand on the beach, spilling pieces of their lives to the tides before the strong currents pulled them under to other shores. He was a kindred spirit, a man who had finally mastered the rhythm to the ticking of Madison's brain. He had saved her, guarded her demons, and buried them with her old life. Too many of the men in Madison's life had left too soon.

The chairs were set in a semi-circle facing the ocean, his urn in the center. Madison stood on the end of the boardwalk as footsteps approached. She wiped a few stray tears before turning around. At twelve, Hannah Beth was almost as tall as Madison. She had long blonde hair and freckles that hinted childhood, but puberty was fast approaching. They embraced and Madison felt small bumps growing on Hannah's girlish chest. Hannah whispered *I love you Momma.* Madison and Hannah conveyed a silent, unspoken intimacy shared only between mothers and daughters. Hannah had issues of her own, demons brought about by Vincent's death. As she looked into Hannah's starry blue eyes, she knew that Rhett would be proud of his very complex daughter.

Lane materialized out of the shadows. She had always appeared like a mist, never feeling worthy of an entrance. Lane squeezed Madison's shoulders in comfort. She whispered *I'm sorry.* Madison kissed Lane, hugging her long, their sobs visible in their shoulders. Hannah watched these two strong, tenacious women become vulnerable, their body language fluid and soft. They had saved Hannah's life, sacrificing pieces their own. Lane reached out her hand to Hannah, admiring the cocooning maturity. Lane studied Hannah's fingers. She wondered the places they would pull her, the lives she'd touch. She was proud of her, yet fearful of her bloodline. Intense therapy had brought Lane through self-loathing, allowing her to move past the lies and blackmail that had become so normal. Yet, the mind games had left their toxic and lasting effects on all involved.

Others from all over had gathered to pay their respects in a separate service. This was a small gathering just for Madison's chosen family. Madison had made her life in Gulf Shores. She found the beach a natural home. She found solace in the cadence of the tides. She even flew a kite without wincing at the tug of the strings.

Madison raised her arm to wave at him when the old gunshot wound sent pains through her shoulder. He was walking the beach, his house only three down. Madison grinned as Dyer's boots threw sand wildly with each labored step. They were the same kind of boots that had walked across Rhett's expensive hardwood floors and square into the middle of her life. Dyer had been badly wounded from raining bullets, had endured months of physical therapy. He was now a contractor along the gulf coast, building new condominiums and beach houses.

Dyer held Madison's slender fingers in his meaty, callused grip. He would never forget their machinations. Their fine tuned chemistry had helped them raise Hannah. They spoke in the space between their bodies. The space that had always been reserved for Hannah was now a blooming garden of trust and kinship. Hannah watched their very intimate interaction, the grief evocative. Dyer kissed Madison's cheek, running his thumb over her faint scar. He released her hand slowly, still finding comfort in her touch. Dyer noticed Hannah staring at them. Hannah knew her father would always reserve a special place for Madison.

Everyone who sat in the semi-circle had seen the many facets of his and Madison's relationship over the years. Each had their own specific recollections.

Madison's life had been stellar with him.
He had been the sunshine in her face,
casting a shadow on the cold, empty years.
There were windows to her heart he opened,
letting the winds of hope entertain her. The
wind still blew her dreams magically in
swirls as only he had promised. He had set
things in motion in her mind and heart.

Madison felt a tug on her skirt. Two
little arms had wrapped around her leg and
he was looking up at her with his heart-
shaped smile.

"Don't cry Momma. Poppa's in
Heaven."

He pointed to the sky with his tiny
finger. She bent down to his level and they
looked into each others' fated eyes. He
smiled like his father, his hair dark like
Houston's. He exuded their love, a
combination of their potential. He opened
his arms, wanting Madison to pick him up.
He was tall for five years old, was getting
too big to lift, especially with her bad
shoulder.

"Come here piano man. I'll carry you."

Houston bent down, lifting Houston Peck King onto his shoulders high above everyone so he could wave at his Grand Poppa in Heaven. Madison put her arms around her husband as their bright star rode his father's strong shoulders.

When they had found out they were having a boy, Houston started calling him "piano man." Peck had been born roughly nine months to the day Houston and Madison had made love on the piano in the Capital Hotel. He had been conceived on that black baby grand. Peck's face was more charming and amorous than most babies'. He personified the romance Houston and Madison had created that full moon midnight. Houston bought that black piano and it now sat in their den. Peck was a regular at banging out his own off-key symphony.

The cork popped on the champagne, silencing their chatter. The cool blue sky turned the beach a purple tint as twilight fell.

264

Everyone moved with vague outlines like ghosts over the sand. The lingering shadows were the ghosts of their lives. Ghosts forever tethered or bound to their minds, chiseling their resolve.

A familiar squeal rose from the end of the boardwalk. Dyer held Peck on his shoulders, bouncing him up and down as he giggled. Hannah braided Lane's long, dark hair. Houston and Madison poured champagne. They all toasted Peck Fleming in celebration. Madison kissed her kite string charm, looking into Houston's insatiable turquoise eyes. He winked at her. A young boy ran the beach, navigating a kite that skirted and flirted with the heavens. He cheered at the volatile trajectory of its flight. His greatest folly found in the uncertainty of the journey.

Monica C. Petter is a poet and

author with seven published books of poetry
and prose. She was a Poet Laureate
nominee for the state of Arkansas. Her
narrative voice is full of vivid language and
metaphor arising from her poetic
beginnings. Monica's diagnosis with
Multiple Sclerosis at age twenty blends the
undercurrents of challenge with emotional
storytelling.

Besides writing, Monica is a photographer
and painter. She lives in Stuttgart, Arkansas
with her husband, David and their lab,
Blondie.